A MODEST DAY'S FISHING

BY

JOHN L DUDGEON

EXCALIBUR PRESS OF LONDON
13 Knightsbridge Green London SW1X 7QL

Copyright © 1992 John L Dudgeon

Printed and bound in UK
Typesetting by CBS Felixstowe Suffolk
Published by Excalibur Press of London
ISBN 1 85634 171 2

To my wife, always a sympathetic listener, as well as to my family and friends whose company has brightened many blank days on the water.

CONTENTS

Introduction

1	Weather Conditions	1
2	State of the Water	11
3	Boats	19
4	Fishing Birds	31
5	A Word of Advice	41
6	Tackle	47
7	Small Fry	57
8	Pause for Food	67
9	Sea Trout at Fourteen	75
10	A Companion on the River	81

INTRODUCTION

"Success is the only invariable criterion of wisdom to vulgar minds."
(Burke)

Among my fishing acquaintances there is one whom, when we meet during the season, I have to congratulate on his most recent achievements.

There is little doubt that he will have succeeded where I have failed. Every year, under a variety of conditions, he has caught numbers of fish of impressive size with reliable regularity. Mutual friends support his claims and, with myself, express unreserved admiration.

I have read in angling publications of others like my acquaintance. Altogether they provide evidence that the efforts of some men at least are properly rewarded. There are detailed figures of what fish they have caught, and when and were exactly. It seems that they have found fish in the particular places where fish were supposed to be. The fishes' preferred food has been unerringly identified, matched and then presented to the water. Trout or, on occasion, salmon have duly come to the cast as planned and, after a sequence of hooking, playing and netting, properly executed, a succession of keepable specimens have been weighed into the bag.

Absolute failure, it seems, rarely occurs and is not considered worthy of mention.

But wherever there is repeated success there sometimes are found the growing cankers of envy, suspicion and discredit. Even angling is not free of these. Thankfully I am not myself at risk in this way, for I have not been overburdened with success, as it is generally measured, in my fishing life.

Instead, my record of catching trout and salmon over half a century has suggested to me that it might now be time to attempt some justification of all the days and countless hours which fishing has occupied for so modest a return. It has been pointed out to me, not unkindly, that a fraction of the same time might have been spent more productively in my rather neglected and unkempt garden, with equal benefit to my health. Alternatively it has been suggested, I might have achieved a more complete relaxation of mind and body by remaining at the water side, without any tackle, watching the coming and going of birds and beasts, admiring small flowers at the lake edge, or writing simple lines of verse.

I like to think that the variety of excuses and apologies for indifferent performance which follow will provide some sort of logical argument on behalf of myself and other anglers who from time to time may have experienced similar doubts and dissatisfaction.

I am certain that, for those people as for me, fishing has always meant something more than the catching of fish and, as the recreation of a lifetime, has continually brought its own intangible rewards.

Weather Conditions

"Blows the wind today and the sun and the rain are flying"
(RL Stevenson)

It is always remarkable to those who are not themselves devoted to angling that there appears to be an invariable optimism about fishermen at the start of any new day's fishing; an optimism which shows little concern for the prevailing weather conditions or for any forecasts regarding its immediate future. Nevertheless the state of the weather lies at the very heart of fishing.

It is also generally felt that conditions of wind, rain and temperature which would drive indoors the most ardent gardeners, cricketers, sailors and even golfers, causing widespread cancellation of fixtures in sporting calendars, will be largely ignored by fishermen. Or perhaps they will be seen merely as an enhanced challenge to them to be out and about their business.

In point of fact, weather conditions which are reckoned bad for other outdoor sports are generally bad for angling also. On the other hand, ideal weather for the golfer, gardener and others is also unsuitable for fishing.

Along with other habitual fishermen I have experienced over the years practically every form of unsuitable weather encountered by those who live in temperate regions. There have been days of incessant downpour, of Wagnerian thunder, of storm force winds, of impenetrable fog, or of unremitting, numbing cold. These have contrasted with other days of flat and blazing hot stillness when boats and fishing lines have floated motionless on mirrorlike surfaces.

If there is any satisfaction to be gained by a fisherman persevering in such circumstances it is that he is provided with a valid excuse for failing to catch fish. If, on the other hand, he has anything at the end of the day to show for his labour then his credit will be greatly increased in the eyes of those who stayed at home.

I recollect a day spent alone on Lough Sheelin many years ago.

The light, south-east breezes of a May morning had dwindled inexorably to nothing during the space of an hour and by lunchtime my boat was floating motionless in mid-lake somewhere between Church Island and Kilnahard shore to the north.

An occasional mayfly, hatched in the shallows around the island, flew steadily and high overhead on its way to final fulfilment amongst hazel bushes and alders which everywhere fringe the water's edge. Far above any risk from hungry trout the 'green drakes' needed only to beware of watchful chaffinches and blackheaded gulls. Lough Sheelin trout resigned themselves to feeding on the bottom.

The sun continued to shine with a brilliance that would have been a blessing to any one but a fisherman. Damp patches left by dripping oars inside the boat grew lighter in colour, dried and vanished. Seats grew hot to the touch. Rowlocks squeaked and groaned dismally whenever I moved the oars. It occurred to me that a greater degree of comfort might be obtained by discarding knee boots and moving myself to the floorboards where I could sit with my back cushioned by a collection of discarded garments.

Two fishermen in another boat some quarter-of-a-mile away seemed already to have done the same thing, for only their heads were visible above the side, motionless in resignation or else asleep. They were the only other people visible on the four mile expanse of lake as I looked around. The day was not, it seemed, one for catching fish.

Another grey-green mayfly freshly hatched from its papery pupa passed softly by, fluttering hard in the still air and intent on making the far-off shore. A moment later and some notion, or an imperceptible current, caused the fly to turn and rise and then to drop again. It lit upon the lake not thirty feet away, the weight of its spread limbs not sufficient to break the surface tension. For several seconds it was poised there, reflected in the water like a tiny yacht with all sails aloft, and then, suddenly it was gone, into a cavern, to the accompaniment of a smooth rolling swirl from which there spread rapidly expanding rings of tiny waves.

A trout had come from the depths to find, just once, its choicest food and having fed was about to sink once more to gravelly beds far beneath.

With a most untidy clatter of oars and of all the tackle which lay around me I snatched my fly rod from the bows and, hastily drawing off several yards of line, cast to the centre of the rippling circles. The trio of wet flies formed a wavy chord across the patterned circle and lay there floating in momentary anticipation.

In another instant the trout rose again. It did not seem to have regard for the threatening shadow or overhanging bulk of the boat or the ropelike line, but seized upon the fly offered to it and turned for home.

There was a splendid moment while the rod bent, the reel spun and the line cut audibly through the water. At the sound of the creel my distant neighbours sat suddenly upright in their boat, their faces turned with an impression of unbelief.

I reeled in. The fish ran out and I reeled again. A great splash on the surface was followed by another deep tugging rush to the bottom. A period of near panic followed when it seemed certain that my line was being taken directly underneath the boat with every likelihood of the trailing flies becoming hooked on the keel.

But my old cane rod continued to spring and bend and to exert its pressure on the fish which presently began to tire. I shook my landing net free from a nail head which held it tight to the bottom boards. Another short run, another reeling, and then that wonderful moment of triumph when having guided the fish to the net I lifted all inboard.

A big trout, my notebook records, weighing almost four pounds. This was fully as much as one could expect to find in good fishing conditions, let alone on a morning of flat calm and blazing sun.

However, most occasions when I have considered the weather to blame for poor fishing are associated with excessive quantities of wind rather than too little. That steady breeze from a southerly or westerly quarter which is traditionally favoured by angling writers may well have followed them on their expeditions. In my experience it has been replaced by near-gales of continually changing strength and direction.

On shore or river bank such conditions are an embarrassment to both a feeding trout and intent angler. A squally gale blowing upstream carries hatching flies together with fishermen's casts high into surrounding trees. The same sort of wind blowing downstream tends to deposit wet fly lines like a haphazard load of coals on top of any fish near the surface.

In a boat, on broad loughs, the effects of high winds are at best laborious for a fisherman and at worst downright dangerous. Experience of big Irish lakes in a variety of weathers has given me a healthy respect for and keen awareness of what can happen when winds get up suddenly.

Reefs and rocky points which provide attractive drifts for the wet fly fisherman on a day of moderate wind become a different matter, and to be treated with extreme caution, in wild weather. Jagged masses lurk in the troughs of four-foot waves or erupt fountains of spray in front of the rocking boat. Sheltered waters are then essential; boats are worked into the lee of wooded islands and either drawn up on shore, whilst the worst passes over, or else headed cautiously for home if the day shows no improvement.

A year or two ago, during a generally deplorable summer, the fringe of a hurricane passed over the mid-west of Ireland at the same time as we were spending our family holiday on and around Lough Melvin. On Monday, following a week-end of frustrating calm, we were greeted by a south east wind of exceptional force which swept the full length of the lough from Rossinver and, with accumulated strength, piled up great ocean-like rollers in Lareen Bay where we were staying. Strong trees along the shoreline waved and bent like reeds whilst the reeds themselves, in their serried ranks, were nearly prostrate in the water, vanishing and rising and vanishing again like a million tiny fishing rods in the surge which swept over them.

The lake narrows at Lareen towards its outflow into the River Drowes. There is a patch of water some three to four acres in area, part river, part lake, which is substantially sheltered from the main lake by a low gravelly spit of land and by deep, dense beds of reeds. Even with the wind and waves roaring and crashing outside, the resilience of the reeds and their density transformed the violent conditions on the lough into a moderate state around the outflow.

My son Timothy and I walked, in a somewhat depressed mood, down to the wall where Tom Gallagher kept his boats, our black plastic coats whipping and flapping around us like a dejected cormorants' wings. Despite their protection from the wall Tom's boats bobbed and shook nervously whenever an exceptional gust sent little waves scurrying under their sterns.

Tim, who is nothing if not optimistic in his fishing, carried a fly rod (permanently assembled while on holiday) with a couple of small wet flies attached. I held my cap on my head to prevent it from vanishing in the direction of the Atlantic some four miles away. Scurrying green leaves torn from nearby sycamore trees swept past us in a little cloud, accompaniment for a struggling crow which shortly gave up the buffeting and sought shelter behind a large rock.

It seemed that this would be a day when weather conditions would protect Melvin trout from any annoyance by anglers.

At this point a trout rose briskly not twenty yards from the stern of the nearest boat. It appeared to be of takeable size. A minute later it was followed by another rise, further out at a place where the current started to speed-up perceptibly towards the throat of the river. Looking east at the more broken water we saw a considerable splash which might have been a good trout or else a dabchick diving. Tim expressed his view that it was a trout and that we should have a try at catching it.

Conditions now, although difficult and uncomfortable for boat fishing, were not likely to be unsafe in the area sheltered by the reeds and I allowed myself to be persuaded. A boat was untied and launched. The reeds shook as it seemed in mockery at our coming and a pair of swans withdrew disdainfully to the far bank where they were joined by a small huddle of storm-tossed mallard.

We did remarkably well, all things considered, during the next hour in that little corner of the lake. Pulling at the oars for two hundred yards into a gale, as far as the margin of reed beds which protected us from the wild water beyond, and then drifting erratically back towards the river we searched out every little corner, rock cluster and clump of weeds where a trout might lie. The water was in some places, as our boat keel proved, only a foot in depth. Further into the channel it was nearly four feet.

Admittedly we had to return two fish for every one we could keep, such was size disproportional to enthusiasm for Tim's flies. There was a three-quarter pound sonaghan trout in the bag, and two gillaroo of similar weight, together with three smaller brown trout. They seemed not particular as to pattern of fly or precision of presentation but rose happily to the surface and took decisively when given a chance. Sometimes our boat blew aground whilst playing fish. Once, line and oar got into such a state of entanglement that the oar rather than the rod was playing a small trout which had attached to itself a mass of trailing weed for good measure.

Wind blew heavily and unceasingly throughout, causing the boat to crab and spin and generally behave like a live thing if ever the oarsman relaxed from his work. When I paused momentarily to point out a jet black mink making its way unconcernedly along the shore twenty yards away we drifted into a combination of wind and current such that fisherman, oarsman, boat, rod and net became bound together with a substantial length of fence and a barrowful of floating rubbish attached to it.

It was all very satisfying, however, if exhausting, and we came safely ashore with an aura of minor triumph and with enough fish caught to display and record and to eat for lunch. The adversity of the weather had been overcome, by perseverance as much as good luck.

The presence of a younger fisherman does of course have a significant bearing on events such as these. For myself, I feel little inclination to start a fishing season before the softer days of April have arrived. Not so many years ago I would have become restless by early March or at least by the middle of that unpredictable month.

There was even a period in my younger days when, with trout fishing opening in February on the River Lagan, I would make early expeditions to the upper reaches of that pleasant stream. Then the only signs of spring were occasional clusters of bright green honeysuckle leaves in sheltered corners and festoons of half-formed catkins in hazel branches over the river. Patches of frost lingered on the grass where no sun had reached and small icicles dripped in dark corners above the water.

I cannot recollect that much was ever caught on the fly in those early-season outings. Only a general impression of cold water and biting little winds remains with me.

I have never been inclined to join the numbers of those who set forth in January to look for an early salmon. (Or could it be a late, late salmon from the previous year?) They are welcome to their numbed extremities, to water frozen in rod rings and to colourless, muddy banks without sign of flower or bird to brighten the day.

Apart from personal discomfort, the coldness of a fishing day, even should it occur at midsummer, is linked more clearly in my mind with failure to catch trout than any other factor. Low temperatures persisting after a chill night or sustained by a northeast breeze seem to get to the fish, to their food and to the angler with equally negative results.

I remember being taught in school that Ireland is subject to a system of prevailing winds from the south and west which are responsible for a soft, damp climate tending to keep loughs and rivers at a proper level throughout the summer.

It seems to me, however, that in recent seasons there has been an increasing predominance of unorthodox weather reaching us from the north and east, particularly in spring and early summer. Chill dry winds have tended to bring with them days of gloomy, grey, unbreaking haze. Such days do not inspire thoughts of fishing in my mind.

I wait instead for a morning when light showers patter softly against the west windows of our house and when light and shade chase each other across the garden and there is warmth enough to open all the crocuses under the shrubbery.

Then I have a feeling that the time has come; that water flies are hatching and fish stirring; and that the only proper place to be is beside a lake or river with my sons or some good friend and strength enough to cast a line again.

State of the Water

"All your better deeds shall be in water writ"
(Beaumont and Fletcher)

Desmond, a long-time non-fishing friend whose patience in my company over many years has been praiseworthy, used to make up for his lack of active participation when we were out together by contributing a selection of comments which he had picked up to sustain me through the day, during which he spent his time reading or walking or sleeping.

He was especially aware, after seeing me on many occasions peer down anxiously from bridges over rivers or scan lake edges as we approached the start, that it was proper to suggest that the water appeared "to be in good order". If my mind was at rest, more or less, on that score the day could at least start on a good note.

Only an angler, I believe, is aware that fresh water, in its natural state, exists in an immense variety of form, composition, and colour even though its condition can seldom be regarded as an ideal one in which to catch fish.

Still water does not offer the same range of variations as does running water and the effects of temperature and wind are principal factors. The clarity of lake water is more often than not related to the growth of algae or to that present day curse of many Irish loughs, eutrophication.

It is hard to believe that twenty years ago Lough Sheelin, for example in County Cavan, beloved of many anglers, was so clear over its limestone bed that one could easily see stones and plants on the bottom at a depth of ten feet. It did not seem to matter that Sheelin trout, in such conditions, could equally well see what was above them when fishing boats cast their shadows overhead.

The water had an intrinsically pure yet living quality. Thirsty fishermen did not hesitate to drink from it without even the precaution of boiling a kettle and on warm days the lake was even an invitation to bathe - if trout were proving unresponsive.

In contrast to Lough Sheelin, as it used to be, there is a twenty-acre dam not far from Belfast where I used to fish, with modest success, at a time when its waters were becoming increasingly affected by seepage from a nearby pig farm. Trout, with which the dam was regularly stocked, were there in adequate numbers and ran to a good size - two pounds or more. It appeared that they existed healthily and happily in the over-rich water which, viewed from above had the appearance of unstirred pea soup - millions of gallons of it.

During a summer's day odds were very much against the likelihood of a team of wet flies crossing the path of any cruising trout, or coming sufficiently close for the flies to be visible at all. Presumably it was more profitable to the fish to grub amongst the gravel and weed roots and feed on larvae, worms and water shrimp. They seemed to grow fat on such a diet.

Only during the late evening, from May onwards, when light started to fade did hatches of duckfly, spinners and, later on, sedges by their large numbers on the surface induce trout to come up from the depths so that they could then perceive the food which was available in abundant quantity.

Under those conditions I found that what had been a hopeless exercise during the day was changed to a more rewarding and exciting business in the gathering dark while bats flickered softly around my head.

Little dimpling rises appeared here and there, first singly and then in clusters in corners of the lake and, later, across its whole surface - wherever the fly hatches were thickest. Sounds of feeding fish could be heard when it was too dark for them to be seen. Sometimes they were close by the boat, sometimes right at the very water's edge where overhanging alder branches made casting impossible.

Sooner or later, through persistent and gentle casting with a small wet fly, amongst the rising fish there would be a take. The little tentative rise would turn immediately into a savage pull and a wild flurry of activity in the black water. Whenever a fish was netted, using touch and feel rather than sight, as likely as not I would find the cast wrapped around it in such confusion that there was little to be done, after unhooking, except bundle all away and find a fresh cast from my pocket book with the aid of a torch. Frustration mingled with excitement until the rise was over or the darkness defeated me.

As regards running water and streams and rivers, I would like to be poetic. A living quality is revealed in so many forms, whether the water runs swift or slow, smooth or broken, rising or falling, dull or sparkling, turning, curling, straightening and turning again.

Infinitely attractive are the colour changes which depend upon depth, on the underlying bed, on a diffusion of light through the water wherever it breaks into falls and rapids, on reflections from above, or the variety of sediment carried in the current.

My favourite streams in the West of Ireland are gold with essence of peat when at normal level, but near-colourless when they drop low in summer. After rain, but only for a few hours at the height of a spate, they become opaque and dirty, and lose something of their charm.

There are, as is well known, narrow limits to the time on such little rivers within which one can be really hopeful of good fishing for sea trout or maybe a salmon, at least during the day. I believe that over the years I have learnt to come to terms with unfavourable fishing conditions and to recognize, those conditions in which the state of the water makes it obvious that the labour of fishing is out of proportion to the chances of catching a fish.

I confess that I am not interested in theories about fishing upstream with a fine cast and a single fly, or even a small pink worm, for an unwary sea trout in low water. In my opinion there are no unwary sea trout, and certainly not in low water.

There is a great deal of pleasure to be had on a river or beside a river, even at those times when one has decided to lean the rod against a tree for an hour or so and use a fishing bag as a support for one's back whilst stretching out weary legs on the grass.

Sons of the family and other young members of the party may happily continue their energetic way, creeping upstream to find a solitary fish still active in the shallow runs. I rest in comfort and listen to the water bubbling around a large rock in front of me reflecting on how cool and refreshing it will be to my feet when I have summoned enough energy to take off socks and waders.

Unfortunately it is not always possible to be so enthusiastic about conditions which prevail at present on rivers in the West of Ireland, and indeed elsewhere in this supposedly civilized country.

Little rivers like the Eanymore and Eanybeg, the Oily, the Stragar, the Yellowater and others draw their life from springs and pools in remote corners of the Bluestack mountains and from those heights they run swiftly down to the Atlantic in Donegal Bay. Joined by myriad other tiny streams and trickles they scour the land of a thousand farms which lie along the north side of the bay.

Every house, shed, shop, garage, even the occasional small factory, is not far from some minor drain, at least, which feeds into one of these rivers.

Thus the rivers are regarded as useful and are made use of accordingly by those who live near them and by others as convenient carriers of rubbish and refuse of all kinds. Much of this refuse, in modern terms, is not of natural origin and will not dissolve or break down with the passage of time or water.

Most conspicuous at water's edge one sees the result of living in the awful age of plastic. It floats, hangs, lurks and obtrudes in a thousand grotesque forms and colours, in obscene contrast with all that surrounds it.

I know of a dozen stretches of supposed fishing water where at any time of the year a full cart load of rubbish could be gathered within less than half-a-mile. Nobody wants to know how it got there and nobody is troubled to remove it.

I fished one such stretch of river on a day in early July, for sea trout which had started to run upstream from the sea pools a few miles below. There had been a series of 'freshes' or small floods occasioned by two or three days heavy, intermittent rain. Four or five miles from the sea a road bridge crosses the river and leads to a junction with another road where there is a small cluster of cottages and a shop. The buildings are not more than a hundred yards from the water, lining the top of an intervening, rushy field.

The river itself bends left handed after it passes under the bridge and then straightens and widens to the extent of a long cast. There follows a flat of moderate depth where trout have always been likely to lie. They can find cover and the sort of privacy which sea trout favour, under an overhang of scrubby birch trees and hazel bushes on the right bank.

Three feet below the gently moving surface flat slabs of rock paving alternate with patches of coarse grained sand. This is overlooked by a high, flat bank on the left side, clear of any growth bigger than an occasional gorse bush and requiring at all times a stealthy approach to the water. It was a delightful place to fish where I knew my way well and felt that I could find a taking fish.

My usual choice of flies would have been for a Golden Olive on the dropper with a small Wye Bug on the tail just in case a salmon might be hovering around in company with its smaller cousins.

And, in fact, there was a salmon there on that particular morning - a very small grilse lying right at the head of the run. As I knelt on the grass and cast across the river practically to the hazel bushes on the far bank the fish rose with bright splashing enthusiasm to seize the gingery lure where it fell as though toppled from the branches.

Exercising restraint I remained kneeling on the bank and therefore substantially out of sight to any fish in the lower part of the run. I have always been aware that a height of over six feet may provide advantages when standing in a crowd but presents extra problems of concealment at the waterside.

Fortunately the little grilse once hooked, stayed within the confines of two table cloths in front of me, and presently I was able to net it with only slight disturbance of the river.

Despite the smallness of my fish - for it weighed only a little over two pounds - I felt a glow of success and that particularly unique expectancy which distinguishes the delight of angling from any other sport.

The best of the water was now ahead of me. It was full of possibility, curling and rippling slightly where an upstream breeze competed with the strength of the current. The gold of the underlying sand was muted darkly by the soft greys of a broken sky overhead. The sun would present no trouble.

Fish were there. I was sure that I saw a heavy sea trout turning close to the surface, twenty feet below where I had been casting. I prepared to cast again.

At that moment there erupted about me a combination of roaring, rattling, sliding, splashing sounds. They came from a point some fifty yards upstream where a dense cluster of hazel bushes obscured my view of the far bank. After a few seconds the noise ceased and there was silence, broken only by a few isolated splashes. The voices of the stream took over again and, with some mystification, I resumed my casting.

As the bob fly on my cast worked attractively towards me on the top of the water it was suddenly joined by a plastic detergent bottle, hideously blue and white, and then by another which danced around it locked in some obscene pas de deux.

A large black plastic bag rolled over and over in the current, on its way downstream, spilling out a part of its horrid contents on each rotation. Half-a-dozen mineral bottles of the largest size in varying degrees of submersion floated like a flock of idiot birds over the nose of the sea trout which I had imagined to be lying in wait for my fly.

To add to the alarm, an entire, but aged, yellow lettuce disintegrated rapidly in mid stream and one substantial leaf attached itself to my tail fly with a dreadful determination.

As a backcloth for the miscellany of glass, plastic and vegetable items which dotted the surface of the little river there now spread through the water a streaky cloud of sinister colour. I could see that it emanated from a number of tins which clattered slowly down the stony bed. What precisely they contained was difficult to determine. Perhaps paint, perhaps some domestic grocery long since deteriorated, or something else more toxic.

In total, the debris made a picture resembling the work of some avant gard artist who sees more virtue in the grotesque and the discordant than in any natural state. The 'artist' in this case, or the creator of the mess which swam before me, was merely an unthinking person who, like too many others, regarded the river only as a convenient dumping place. Aesthetic or sporting values were of little importance.

Water is an element taken for granted in Ireland: there is a very great deal of it around in lake and river. It seems to cost nothing. Regrettably, its ready availability is taken as a reason for paying scant attention to care of its purity or preservation, for now or for the future.

Boats

"To be imprisoned in the viewless winds
And blown with restless violence round about
The pendant world"
(Shakespeare: 'Measure for Measure')

A boat is for the angler an aid to the catching of fish. Its use is therefore not to be thought as any sort of recreation, as an opportunity for exhibitions of oarsmanship, navigation skills or even athletic heroics in the event the weather turns bad.

Generally, the speed with which an angler's boat covers a given distance on water is less important than the manner in which it does so. Having regard to natural hazards, the desirability of keeping reasonably dry and comfortable inboard and a degree of stealth and quiet where feeding fish are about are what count.

Sometimes a boat is absolutely essential for a day's fishing, as when large bodies of water would otherwise be totally inaccessible. By casting from the shore of an Irish lough, even with the longest of lines and the longest of waders, it is still impossible to reach trout who can judge precisely how closely they may feed with safety along the water's edge.

At the same time it is remarkable how often one sees fishermen, who have put themselves to the trouble of embarking on a large lake, persist in staying on the water closest to the land. They risk collision with every outlying rock and even entanglement with the branches of overhanging trees in order to attend to those fish which prefer the shallow waters. They know, of course, that many trout, at certain times of day or condition of wind, will happily stay where a variety of food falls from trees or bushes, washing out from drains and streamlets and being blown in again with every breaking wave.

As to the boat itself, if well designed and of proper size and shape for fly fishing, it should fit around fishermen almost as well as a coat and be sensitive to direction at a touch of the oar. This is still important even in the present day when sophisticated outboard motors have not only largely eliminated the heavy physical work required to move from drift to drift in a fresh wind but are increasingly employed to shift a boat backwards or forwards from fish to fish or in responding quickly to any change of mind on the part of the angler.

Like other fishermen I have experience of many different conditions of boats. The nature of my experience has been due to having to manage them myself, or with my friends, rather than relying upon the services of a professional boatman. Nowadays, despite their undoubted value on occasions, boatmen constitute a very substantial and avoidable additional on-cost to the day's fishing.

On reflection it would be true to say that whilst the characteristics and behaviour of boats from which I have fished have seldom had much effect on the weight of the bag they have had a profound effect on how I felt at the end of a day.

Size of boat is of course a prime factor. There must be enough space to allow for normal moving about and free casting for two, or it might be three, grown men, without hindrance. There must be enough length, keel and beam to stay reasonably steady and safe amongst the heavy 'seas' which can be encountered on Loughs such as Mask or Erne or Conn.

I recall occasions when, for various reasons, boats did not appear to be big enough to meet the day's needs.

For example: on a day some years ago I joined two friends to fish for pike in Lower Lough Erne. John and his father, 'The Major' who owned a ten foot glass fibre dinghy, had brought this with them on the roof of their car to Drumgrenahan Bay, to meet me there. That part of the Lough, as some will know, lies on the south facing shore of Boa Island and is easily accessible by a road which sixty years ago was built to join the island to the mainland.

The bay although half-a-mile wide at it's mouth is shallow and sheltered from the main lough by overlapping wings of Lusty Beg and Cruninish islands which break up any big swell sweeping across from Magho mountain and the West Fermanagh hills.

Nevertheless with a stiff breeze in that quarter likely to make hard work for the oarsman, we proposed not to venture much outside the bay but rather confine ourselves to trolling to and fro within its limits.

We are, each of us, six feet tall, and built as they say in proportion, so that together in the dinghy our appearance must have been something like the three unfortunates who in the nursery rhyme set forth in a tub.

Casting or throwing a spoon bait in any direction had to be done with care, having regard to the trim of the boat as well as the nearness of other occupants. Any unheeding strokes on the short oars were liable to be painful for the man sitting astern. We felt ourselves always to be extremely close to the water level. We had two short trolling rods at work and I know that the bait on one of them was an ancient fiddle-back spoon which my father had made, painted black on one side and dull copper on the other. We trailed this from one side of the bay to the other, two or three times in succession, finishing at the eastern side where the water deepens under the shadow of a rocky, scrub-covered point. Even there it was not easy to keep triangle hooks clear of the lake bottom, particularly when the boat was being turned to repeat its previous course. After several pulls and jerks from weeds and stones, which were quickly cleared, the spoon stuck firmly and finally. Line ran out astern as fast as the dinghy was rowed. John, who was at the oars, slackened pace and the clicking of the reel slowed in turn. All was still while I applied tentative pressure in a to clear the snag. The Major wound in his line to prevent the second spoon from being lost on the bottom. John then set about taking us to deeper water in the centre of the bay.

At that moment the top of the rod bent in a dramatic arc and shook violently while line ran from the reel in a convulsive rush. The point where it vanished into the water moved swiftly from dead astern to one far out on the port side. There it paused for a few seconds before departing once more, heavily and irresistibly towards the bows. It was apparent that we were attached to a large fish which was encircling us like some menacing submarine.

Now it came towards us on the starboard side rising gradually all the time until suddenly there was a massive swirl on the surface. We had a momentary glimpse of fins, a marbled, mottled flank and a great wolf-like jaw armed with teeth which snapped closed on the wire trace before the fish vanished once more under the waves. It continued to circle us at a distance of some twenty to thirty yards, so close to the top at times that we could see its tail fin part uncovered like the sail of some small yacht.

When pressure from the rod and reeling-in of line seemed at last to be having some effect and were working the fish nearer to our boat, we began to consider the relative size of each.

The prospects of being joined suddenly in a small, crowded dinghy by a pike of over twenty pounds weight with teeth and an ill temper to match was unattractive, even if we could manage to get it inboard in the first place. It was decided that we should row steadily for the shallows and settle events on shore rather than afloat.

Under the Major's direction John put his back into the oars and while I sat astern holding rod aloft the pike was - in its more amenable moments - towed behind us like a calf.

In a foot of water we all quit the dinghy and I was given the honour of continuing with the rod. John picked up an ancient salmon gaff from the bottom of the boat and waited for the pike to be brought within striking distance.

Presently, in response to pressure, it cruised smoothly past us, a small bow wave rippling at its nose and its back fins barely awash. A firm, decisive stroke with the gaff, a tremendous thrashing splash at our feet, sending water over us in showers, and the pike departed at top speed towards the centre of Drumgrenaghan Bay with the reel spinning and the head of the gaff in the fish's side while John was left to examine the broken shaft remaining in his hand.

Remarkably, the pike remained attached and, growing weary, was once more persuaded to the shallows, closer and closer to the edge until finally it rolled onto it's side in six inches of water. At that point John and his father abandoned all finesse and wading to the lakeward side of the fish made a combined onslaught to roll and bundle it out of the water on to dry land where it was sharply dispatched with a solid stick.

As trout fishermen by inclination we regarded the removal of any large pike from Lough Erne with satisfaction. In fact, when subsequently cleaned, this particular fish was found to contain, only partially digested, remains of a trout between two and three pounds in weight.

Later in the day we called at a local butcher's to borrow his weighing scales which showed our pike to be twenty-two pounds - after several hours drying out.

Whilst the proper size of a boat is vital in relation to the comfort and convenience of anglers, even more important to their peace of mind is its general condition and state of repair.

Hired boats, when you first find them at the start of a day, may be filled with water. This can be a good sign if it follows a night's heavy rain, suggesting that if the hull is sound enough to keep a substantial amount of rain water inside then, conversely, it should be able to keep the lake water out, once properly afloat. On the other hand there may be unseen splits and cracks of such magnitude that the lake courses freely in and out until it finds its own level. In general any oldish boat, unless you have owned it and cared for it yourself and know its full history, is always suspect.

Water lobelia is an attractive and common little plant which grows at the edge of many boggy Irish lakes. Its mauve, violet-like flowers nod gently in sheltered bays and corners above a neat rosette of leaves. I believe its seeds float from place to place so that it can spread wherever there is water and peaty soil in the right combination.

I recollect, however, finding a little colony of these plants flourishing amongst the bottom boards of a timber boat offered me for hire on a Donegal lake. Small, brisk earthworms crawled from joints in the planks when I poked tentatively with my finger nail. An overall coat of fresh blue paint, inside and out, did little to restore my confidence or willingness to contract with the owner for a day on the lake, and it was one of those occasions when I preferred to fish from the shore.

In fact, most boats for regular hire to anglers in these days are maintained in reasonable condition by owners who know their business and value their clientele. Old boats and damaged boats are removed from service and those which are on offer are properly appointed, with matching oars, rowlocks, rope, baling cans (for rain water?) and even, perhaps, a lifebelt as a pessimistic afterthought.

I stayed with my family, during a recent summer, at a small hotel on the west coast of Scotland. The district was one where, it might have been supposed, the ways and needs of trout fishermen would be well appreciated.

The view from our bedroom window, looking across an arm of the sea towards the Cuillin mountains, was magnificent; hospitality was charming, and the food provided by the chef-owner was excellent. Only the trout fishing - the main reason for our stay - was a disappointment.

With insufficient rain to bring sea trout into any neighbouring rivers, the hotel boasted, nevertheless, sole rights of fishing on an "excellent" brown trout loch in the mountains some miles away. Precise information was obtained as to the route to this loch, and glowing, if vague, accounts were given of the quality of fishing to be anticipated. There was even a generous removal of any limit on the bag for the day on account of our failure with the sea trout. To heighten the general level of expectation, and in particular consideration of my wife who was the non-fishing member of our party, enthusiastic reference was made by management to the abundance of golden eagles, otters and wild cats which would most likely add to our entertainment amongst the mountains.

Special reference was made to the boats available on the loch: there were two of these hidden in a little bay in the south-east corner. We were to take the "new" boat, it being the better of the two, and it would be found moored out in the water, at the end of a long line, safe from interference by the unauthorized. A key was provided to unlock chain and padlock so that the boat could be drawn in to the land. Oars, rowlocks and baling can were all set carefully at hand, apparently, under a specified turf bank.

We were despatched with thermos flasks and good wishes for our success and the request: "please be sure to leave the boat just as you find it."

In the event we had no difficulty in complying with the last part of the instructions since we were unable to disturb the number one boat in any way from where we ultimately found it. It lay, indeed, some twenty feet out from the boggy shore but resting so securely on the bottom of the lake that only a few inches of the bow showed above water. It was impossible to tell whether the hull was holed or split or simply filled to the brim with a summer's succession of rainfall.

The oars, lying randomly along the water's edge, were as widely assorted in length and shape as a half set of golf clubs and about as usefully designed to propel any boat across the lake. From the assortment we selected two which had a rough similarity in length and a sufficient area of blade remaining. One had a leather collar to hold it in the rowlock, the other had none.

The second boat, lying on dry land, was seemingly sound enough, of glass fibre construction, shallow in draft and sufficient in length to accommodate my two sons and myself. Of the three seats, one lay loose in the bottom accompanied by other unidentifiable fragments of wood.

After both sons had spent twenty minutes baling-out we were able to launch the boat and set about fishing, taking two fly rods and a net. With some trepidation, I elected to row for a start while my sons prepared to cast their choice of Zulus, Clarets and Mallard and whatever else was considered to be in fashion for mountain trout.

We would probably have made reasonable progress in a light breeze, or even a moderate one, but squalls approaching gale force were now developing from the direction of the sea and they whirled around us and over us, sending cluster after cluster of black wavelets scurrying across the loch.

I know when I am enjoying my boating and when I am not. There is little pleasure and little chance of catching fish when one's boat spins like a weather vane at every puff of wind. With little keel and with only an apology for a set of oars to exercise control, our lines, if cast out on the port side were in a moment over-run by the boat, either getting entangled with the blades or in imminent danger of fouling underneath.

A few seconds' relaxation in laborious rowing would result immediately in all way being lost and we would skim downwind as fast as though we had set sail.

When one has to pull hard at oars it is necessary to find a firm purchase point for the feet. In that particular boat there were, however, no traces of a footrest amongst the miscellany of bits which rattled around the bottom. With my feet sliding on the smooth surface of the fibre glass hull I was restricted to short stabs at the water instead of using back and legs to produce a classic stroke.

Colin astern of me and Tim in the bows were lacking in sympathy and found conditions little to their liking so far as catching fish was concerned. Frequent change of direction by the boat while drifting, coupled with the shortness of distance between them, where they sat, tended to produce occasions of mutual entanglement.

Spirited comments on the quality of each other's casting swept past my ears on the wind, together with their flies. I was glad to have secured the hood of my fishing jacket tight around my head.

Colin did not enjoy receiving the occasional sharp blow from an oar or a foot while I struggled with the dinghy. Tim had discovered one or two projecting edges on his seat which had a persistent attraction for slack loops of line. It was while clearing one of these, and with concentration momentarily distracted from the water, that the only trout of the day was seen to rise: something around the length of a moderate-sized teaspoon, we thought.

Conditions became even less pleasant. Heavy rain had joined the squalls of wind and swept in curtains across the bare turf banks where I hoped that my wife was finding more shelter than we were enjoying.

A definite leak had developed, water now making its way steadily into the boat through some unseen crack. There was a need to bale as well as to row and to fish. A picnic bag beneath our feet was becoming more and more saturated.

At last my sons decided that they had had enough and from the end of the remotest bay where the wind had carried us, they took over the oars while I gratefully sat astern. The boat sped with impressive, if spasmodic energy, across a loch speckled all over with white horses. Spray flew from bows and oar blades and I speculated on the likelihood of one or both oars snapping before we made the distance to our mooring.

Eventually, however, and avoiding the sunken boat which, if possible, seemed now even deeper under the waves, we landed in the lee of the bank where we had started and thankfully clambered out. My wife was still there damply studying her bird reference book and with cups of hot coffee poured out ready for us.

It was a measure of the day's failure to come up to its promise that the only wildlife which she had been able to observe throughout the day's wind and wet was a small jenny wren which was in sole possession of the black lochside and which scolded her persistently, unperturbed by any threats from golden eagles, or wildcats.

Fishing Birds

"...or underneath the barren bush
Flits by the sea blue bird of March"
(Tennyson)

The kingfisher is not, in fact, a particularly favourite bird of mine. Its halcyon appearance is spectacular and its efficiency in catching fish unquestionable, but I have always felt that the colours are too strident to be associated with the soft shades of Irish countryside. This, together with the bird's unmusical call, and its preference for muddy, murky stretches or water has always been unattractive to me.

By "fishing birds" I refer to those kinds which have been particularly linked with days spent on my fishing excursions, rather than notable catchers of fish.

I have always enjoyed the sighting of a dipper while on a river. Busy, bobbing and wren-like it has a nicer choice of surrounds than the kingfisher: clear, fast-flowing streams with gravel beds, circling pools and large rocks on which it can perch and watch and wait. Dippers seem to bob in time with their intention to depart immediately but, if the distance between us is sufficient, the bird may stay around while I fish, and even observe me catch a trout.

Birds deserve a chapter, I feel, in any book which attempts to describe the complete pleasures of angling. They belong, after all, to lakes and rivers and wet places almost as much as do the fish themselves. Awareness of their presence has been inseparable for me from the experience of each season's fishing.

If I were to make a list of my most-liked sorts of bird it would certainly contain a high proportion of those which customarily live with wet feet: curlew, snipe, sandpiper, dipper and heron - as well as the ducks and divers which are to be found in fresh water in the West of Ireland during spring and summer.

On a family fishing excursion my wife generally sees interesting birds before I do. It may be necessary for me to adjust my spectacles, or wipe them clear of raindrops, but I still claim to be quicker to identify birds by their call or song.

Common snipe have always held a special fascination for me because of their eery 'bleating' heard high around lakesides on early summer days. Now, I have difficulty in seeing the bird rising and falling in distant flight, making that strange unbird-like sound. Nor can I easily detect a solitary bird perched on a post or stump whilst uttering its sharp warning 'chack-chack' to its mate nesting in the grass below.

Curlews, thankfully, appear to be with us always throughout the season in Ireland. In company with many other anglers, I suppose, I have come to consider a curlew's bubbling cry to be the most evocative of all bird sounds - incredibly wistful and unforgettable. Rarely have I been so absorbed in pursuing fish but that I could find time to look up when a curlew calls and passes by.

Visiting birds, which come to this country only in summer, have a special attraction about them, due in many cases to their diminutive size and their apparent fragility when compared with the great distances which they have travelled to reach here. The inevitability of their going again even before the fishing season is ended demands appreciation of their company while we have it.

Bird experts suggest that nearly half-a-million willow wrens come to these islands every summer. On a May morning on Lough Mask, from a hundred yards off-shore, it would seem, from the collective noise, that the country's full quota of small, cheerful, olive-brown birds has gathered in bushes at the lake edge to call greetings to me and other passing anglers.

Amongst my most memorable 'fishing birds' were undoubtedly the wood warblers which we used to see on visits to Lough Eske in May and June. At the time of our first encounter my elder son and I were in Scott Swan's boat a short distance out from the wooded Ardnamona shore. We were drifting gently across the mouth of Wood Bay, which has always been populated with native 'brownies' and occasional early sea trout.

My wife and younger son were, meanwhile, pursuing a parallel course through the lakeside trees, where we caught glimpses of them when they came close to the water's edge.

They found the wood warbler's territory amongst a group of oak trees and from the boat Colin and I could hear hushed conversation mingling with bird song which was at that time strange to us. Drifting across the water the notes were reminiscent of some parts of a nightingale's refrain but with the addition of distinctive phrases and repetitions.

We paddled the boat through an intervening reed bed and landed quietly in an area of massive, moss-covered boulders shaded by spindly ash and rowan trees. Inland, some fifty yards of less, were the taller oak trees, crept over by ferns and lichen in their lower branches and rising to a translucent canopy of freshly opened green-gold leaves. Up there the male bird was singing and moving ceaselessly from branch to branch, undisturbed by our presence. Its colour was as fresh and delicate as the new leaves: olive above and cream beneath, with a clearer yellow eye stripe than on any other warbler I had seen before.

While we stayed in that place, beneath the trees, the singing continued and the wood warbler remained near us, in an area not much larger than a tennis court. Somewhere was its hidden nest and mate in busy occupation.

We have returned there in two or three recent years at the same time, and on each occasion the wood warblers have been in occupation. Each time I could hear the song a little way out in the lake, whenever the rustle of water quietened or a breath of wind blew the sound towards me from the wooded shore.

Lough Eske, being only a few miles from the sea, and having a variety of cover provided by its scrubby glens and broad-leaved woods, also attracts an assortment of those birds which like to take their share of small trout and char from the lake. Cormorants breed, or attempt to breed, every year on O'Donnell's Island at the south end of the lough, making it noisome and unattractive to anglers who would like to land for lunch. The crumbling walls of a seventeenth century prison on the island, mostly hidden by an over-growth of sycamore and fir trees, are bespattered by a colony of those unwelcome birds, which have few redeeming features to compensate for their large consumption of fish. I am in agreement with those who would reduce the number of cormorants resident around Ireland's lakes and rivers. There is at present an imbalance of cormorant population affecting other fish-seeking birds as much as it does anglers.

Apart from this point, I have always been content to share fish and fishing with the variety of water birds which one encounters every season. However, it is true that after a number of days of less than successful fishing on the waters of Lough Eske I have been inclined to reflect on the greater rewards which the local herons, grebes, ducks and others seem to enjoy for their efforts.

I remember particularly one unusual bird, a great northern diver according to our reference book, which appeared one summer in the corner of Castle Bay. On several occasions during our holiday we were able to watch its sleek shape circling distantly around our boat. If at any time we approached too near the big bird would arch its snake like neck and vanish noiselessly beneath the waves, not surfacing again until it had doubled the space between us.

In fact I cannot recall any moment when we saw the diver with a fish of its own catching, or making any obvious attempt to get one. However, an acquaintance who had spent as much time on the lough as I, over the same period, had an opportunity to form an opinion as to the bird's appetite for trout, and he told me of his experience.

The better part of one July morning had been spent by my friend in close company with the diver, which was apparently attracted more to his solitary presence than to our family boat. A busy hour or two of fly fishing in the sandy corners of the bay had resulted in a collection of some half-dozen trout, of herring size, which the fisherman had arranged neatly along the bottom boards of the boat. There he could admire their golden sides and multi-shaded speckles while continuing to row and cast his line.

The great northern diver stayed twenty to thirty yards away for much of the time, observing each trout being caught, silent as the fish themselves, yet moving as smoothly through the lake as ever they had done. Its bright red eyes followed the splash and flurry which every fish made until brought safely to the net.

So constant and unwavering remained the bird's attention throughout and so hypnotic became the effect of its ceaseless patrol before him that the angler at last gave up his work and rowed to the nearby shore. There, leaving boat, tackle and fish at the water's edge he walked the short distance to his car where his wife was waiting.

Five minutes later they were both back at the boat. A series of rippling arrows spread behind the diver as, seeing them approach, it moved slowly outward though still not going more than a few oars' lengths away. From there it watched them steadily and my friend maintains that he saw one ruby eye in the dark, sleek head, close momentarily and open again as if to convey some secret, humorous message.

There were no longer a half-dozen trout in the boat. Only three remained of the catch and those lay exactly as they had been, unmarked and undisturbed.

I shared the amusement when told shortly afterwards of the vanishing fish but with the passing of time I have felt less certain as to the real identity of the culprit.

Large water birds such as divers, cormorants or grebes are not by any means nimble when out of their preferred element. Getting from the water into a small, steep-sided boat would present problems only likely to be overcome with much flapping, splashing and scrambling likely to be heard, if not actually seen, from some distance away.

More stealthy and silent in its movements, and nearly as agile in water as in land, is that unpopular little animal the naturalised mink. As on many other fresh water loughs and rivers in the West of Ireland the mink, once farmed for its fur, is known to live and breed in hidden lairs amongst tree roots and rocks around the shores of Lough Eske. Preying ferociously on other small animals as well as birds and fish, mink are never far away when unprotected food is available. A bag of freshly caught trout would offer a welcome meal not to be neglected.

A swift leap into the boat and then out again, one fish at a time: a few minutes more and the entire catch could have been removed to the secrecy of neighbouring jungles of fern and hazel bushes.

No doubt the diver must have watched the theft of the trout in every detail. To its mind it would have seemed that, like any other prey, the fish belonged in the end to who ever had the strength and opportunity to take them. There is little sense of ownership in nature!

Bird watchers probably consider that they experience peaks of excitement equal to those of anglers, although their objectives are very different. The sighting of a rare bird in the wild provides moments of awareness and uncertainty, followed by conviction or disappointment, which have parallels in the rising, hooking and landing (or losing) of a good fish. When a bird is both beautiful as well as being unusual, the same sense of achievement is felt by a bird watcher to that of a successful angler.

As a family, we remember *our* osprey on Lough Eske as an event to be counted amongst other memorable experiences of many fishing holidays.

Where our particular osprey came from and where it went after we saw it we never knew. I believe that Lough Gartan also in County Donegal, was being visited occasionally by solitary migrants from Scotland at the time of our sighting.

I use the pronouns 'I' and 'we' rather freely because, in fact, I personally did not see the eagle at all. At the time of the event I was searching instead for sea trout in McAnulty's Bay, half way up the west side of the lough and was temporarily out of sight of my family who were walking the lakeside lane which leads to Ardnamona woods. Between us was a small headland covered with tall pine trees and so, regrettably, I saw nothing of what was visible to the others at that time.

My wife had been watching a pair of reed buntings which were busily engaged in feeding their young in the shelter of a clump of willows close to the lane. There was a general bustle of small birds all around, for it was the kind of bright, fresh, lively day in early July when weather conditions encourage something of a revival of activity and birdsong of two months earlier, when courting and nest-building were in full swing.

Suddenly, however, this particular morning, a silence fell upon the buntings and they and other small birds ceased to move about.

A moment later a dark shadow swept across the waters of the bay beside them. It was followed by a school of swallows, chattering and scolding, swooping and diving in frenzied belligerence. The shadow paused for an instant a short way out where waves started to ruffle in the offshore breeze. It moved a few feet and paused again, like the projection of some small cloud but with a life and motion of its own.

The watchers looked up and there, fifty feet above the lake, hanging and swaying in the sunlight, was a splendid bird, straight from the paintings of Thorburn or Seaby.

The osprey was unmistakeable by its size, its angled wings and its downturned white head scanning the rippling water below. For minutes it seemed oblivious to the ceaseless mobbing of the small birds around it.

Then, as though further to prove its proud identity, the eagle, hovering with fanning wings, checked, sideslipped through the air and plunged like a stone to the lake with outstretched legs and feet. It caused a tremendous splash, sending spray flying and an instant later rose on heavily flapping wings - but without a fish in its talons.

The swallows resumed their mobbing and the osprey resumed its watchful hovering. Despite its size and its deadly talons and beak the great bird could be heard chittering in annoyance at their ceaseless attentions. After a few more minutes, observed in fascination by my family beneath, and deciding that peace was more attractive than the chance of a fish the eagle swung away with rapid wing beats to a straggling fir tree which overlooked another arm of the lough, half-a-mile away.

Even there the prospects of finding food must have been less certain than continuing harassment by its neighbours. Shortly afterwards the osprey left its position on the fir and, rising high over the north end of the lake, it flew steadily towards the highest slopes of the Tawnawilly mountains where it was soon lost from sight against grey slabs of rock and dark sweeps of heather.

A Word of Advice

*"Advice is seldom welcome and those who need
it the most always want it the least"*
                                    (R L Stevenson)

My wife seldom risks giving any advice to me on technical aspects of fishing when we are out together. She contents herself instead with drawing my attention to various incidentals of the day which she knows I would like to hear about and which could affect my success or enjoyment: the rise of a good trout outside my vision; the presence of a thorn bush close to my back cast; the imminence of the water level lapping over my boot tops; the intent of cattle advancing across a field behind me - these are all within her scope.

As a tribute to her assistance I ought to record an instance of unusual and useful advice which she was able to give me not long ago on a family visit to Lough Eske.

It was early in the summer, too early for all but the most precocious of sea trout to enter the lake, and too late for most of the spring-running salmon. Our concern was with the native population of small, hardy brown trout with which the lake has always been well endowed and which are active, generally, throughout the season.

My elder son, then aged ten, and I were together, drifting

slowly in Scott Swan's handy little boat up the west shore of the lake. We were in the midst of an area of rocky reefs and sandy shallows which are partly shaded over by a stand of tall fir trees set close along the water's edge. Between us and the main spread of the lough was a series of exposed stone clusters, the largest topped with a few straggling bushes and known locally as Pigeon Island.

Colin had acquired reasonable ability in casting a line. If placed at the stern of the boat with his light eight-foot rod and given a fair sweep of unobstructed water in front he could address the problem of fishing a fly quite effectively and with little danger to himself or to others around.

He lived in hourly hope of hooking something larger than the half-pound trout which had been his best reward up to that time. In company with his brother he had shared the traumatic experience of being in the boat with me several weeks earlier when I had hooked and eventually landed a small spring salmon. Despite the alarms of that occasion it had registered in his mind as the peak of achievement possible in angling.

The other half of my family were, meanwhile, more or less abreast of us exploring the shoreline on foot, making slow and rather painful progress over moss-grown boulders, through thickets of briar and bramble to a place where a fallen larch tree lay full length across the water, supported by branches part-buried in the sandy bed of the lake.

Occasional small trout made circles on the surface between us and the tree. I paddled the boat towards them while Colin continued to offer for their interest a 'hare's ear' pattern - his own choice for the day.

The trout, however, remained sullen and unmoved for so long a period that thoughts of going ashore to join the others for a spell of bird nesting and a mug of tea became increasingly attractive. Tim, now out of sight in the undergrowth, had apparently found a pair of gold crests and was tracking their progress bush by bush.

I saw my wife standing alone, close to the lake edge, beside the larch tree and peering down intently, with shaded eyes at a point beneath her where rocky ledges descended into some three feet of water before giving way to level coarse sand. Presently she was joined by Tim and both of them considered what she had found.

An instant later they called to us in considerable excitement. It seemed, so far as we could understand, that two fish were swimming slowly past them where they stood, and plainly visible over the sandy bottom. One fish was very big (my wife indicated with outspread hands) and the other not quite so big (another measurement), but both were something exceptional, it appeared.

I was required to row the boat in close at once so that we could cast where my wife showed us. Colin became as excited as the others and implored me to hurry my very best. Keeping silent as to the likelihood of dark, sinuous tree roots in the water, or even their shadows, being mistaken for swimming fish I bent my back to the oars.

There was a little stony promontory for which I aimed in order to land my son, together with his rod, so that he could follow his mother's direction. At least he would be safe there to cast without entanglement in bushes, and hopefully without going bodily into deep water.

It seemed scarcely important to me to observe at the time that the strength of his cast was only intended for trout and that there was but a thirty-yard length of line on his reel.

I then backed the boat away from the stones and rowed out a sufficient distance to reach the off-shore breeze so that my own line would be covered by a moderate ripple. The others gathered together, freed from any critical presence and like a cluster of cormorants continued to gaze earnestly into the waters of the lake, with Colin casting exactly where he was directed.

Suddenly all three combined in a shout which might have been heard on the tops of the neighbouring Bluestack mountains. I looked up to see my son, pale with emotion, clutching a rod which was bent into a semi-circle and with the line running taut to a point a boat's length away, below the surface.

More than ever convinced that a solid tree root or a concealed rock was at the bottom of it all I nevertheless dropped my own rod and scurried towards the action, calling out instructions to all concerned. Colin was by now frozen in a state of ultimate anxiety. My wife was optimistically brandishing our very small landing net and Tim was dancing from stone to stone encouraging his brother in any way he knew how.

With the fly rod now taken into my own hand it seemed certain that the hook was indeed stuck fast in the bottom of the lough. For a full minute resistance was implaceable and the rod remained bent like a hoop.

Then, mysteriously, but with an awful weight, the bottom of the lake withdrew from us infinitesimally, reel click by reel click; an inch, another inch, a foot and then another foot away.

A fish had indeed been hooked and, by our standards, it must be a very large fish. I returned the rod to its owner and secretly offered up a short prayer.

Unwinding slowly, but with a dreadful persistence, line stripped steadily from the reel until plainly only a very few yards remained. The matter was about to end. Taking the rod again I waded out as far as possible for there was no time to return to the boat.

Incredibly the fish stopped at the last controllable moment and then gently returned towards us so that the line could be recovered coil by coil, until I was once more able to pass the rod to Colin.

Backwards and forwards and circling round and round the little bay, sometimes coming close to where we stood, the fish continued its course several times, but always remaining within the ambit of the rocky point and the fallen tree. There were no grand flourishes on the surface, no dramatic leaps or frantic rushes which would quickly have ended the contest. Its exact size could only be guessed at from momentary glimpses of a dark shape when it came close, or a glimpse of silver where a beam of sunlight struck down through the water.

It seemed essential now that we should at least have a clear sight of what Colin had hooked, before he lost it. There should be no weary reflections afterwards as to what its size might have been, and therefore, he applied pressure with his rod which had never before been put to such a test. With only the shortest of lines he was able to guide the fish past us as though it was a dog on a tenuous lead.

I took the landing net from my wife - and it seemed as adequate to the situation as a tennis racquet - and waded resolutely into the lake until water flowed freely over the tops of my thigh boots.

On came the fish towards us, slow and massive. I pushed the net cautiously into its path. Under strain from the rod and the slender cast a salmon rose to the top of the lake and with more hope than confidence I lifted the net handle. Almost gratefully, it seemed, the fish tumbled head and shoulders through the mouth of net and stayed there unmoving, an inert silver bar which we carried before us on to dry land.

My growing suspicions of the past few minutes were realised. We had in fact caught a spent salmon, or kelt, recovered from spawning so that it shone almost as bright as a fresh-run fish. However, instead of the nine or ten pounds which it must have weighed in the previous autumn our lean-flanked captive was not likely to exceed six pounds at the most.

In a way, after the drama of finding, hooking and playing the salmon, I believe that there was some relief amongst the family that it turned out to be as it was - unkeepable and therefore unkillable.

Once the small hook had been carefully removed from the corner of its jaw the fish was returned, very gently to the lake. There supported right way up, two pairs of hands flapped a current of water into its mouth and out through its gills. After a minute or two of this refreshing treatment the salmon gave several faint strokes with its tail and then, imperiously shaking aside the supporting hands, it cruised slowly away into deeper water until lost from sight.

There, perhaps, it was rejoined by its smaller companion and together, we hoped, they may have made their way down the outflowing river to the sea a few miles away.

I remember just about that time the wind changed direction. Instead of blowing off shore, as it had been, it now blew irregularly from the south so that we could feel its strength where we sat on the grass. A cool gust crept across the water.

As with a curtain over an empty stage broken water covered the bay even under the branches of the larch tree. Above us a soft rustle amongst the tree tops made a sound as of faint applause.

Tackle

"...and their net brake..."
                                    Luke Ch. 5 v. 6

I must admit that the misuse of landing nets on my part, as well as their own occasional misbehaviour, has caused me some embarrassment and the loss of good fish in past years. Sometimes the fault was entirely my own, as for example on a day by a Donegal river when I forced a heedless way through a succession of thorn hedges with the net hanging from one shoulder thus proving at the end that blackthorn branches are stronger than flax cord. Later on in the day, because a single mesh had become enlarged to the size of three or four together, the resultant hole proved big enough to allow a pound trout to slide easily through until, hanging suspended by the bob fly for a moment, it shook its way back to the water and freedom.

In general, however there is such a sophistication and degree of technical excellence available in modern fishing tackle that, provided one is prepared to pay enough and to be sufficiently selective when shopping, there is little to be feared from the failure of equipment once a fish has been found and securely hooked. With the replacement of flax by terylene, silk by nylon and cane by carbon fibre, odds rest substantially on the side of fisherman rather than fish. I think that only the present-day scarcity of trout and salmon in relation to the large numbers of people bent on their pursuit and capture can be excuses for our failing to equal catches made by the expert anglers of one hundred or even fifty years ago - the Skues and Halfords, Sheringhams and Taverners who operated with crude equipment, of uncertain performance, doubtful strength and relatively short life.

Reliability is the key word when selecting fishing tackle: a reasonable certainty that each item will perform in use exactly as it has been claimed to do by the supplier; and that it will continue to do so in a variety of testing conditions long after leaving the shop or showroom. But with fishing tackle more than with any other sport's equipment, it remains the owner's vital responsibility to take proper care of what he has bought or been given. Neglect or the imposing of unfair demands are factors which frequently account for minor disasters on the day.

I shall never be allowed to forget an incident of this kind which occurred on the river Eanymore about ten years ago. It was immediately after a late September flood in the river and I had made my way to Drumboarty Bridge where a deep pool known locally as 'The Sandhole' was always a favoured resting place for grilse, and where even a stale salmon might be persuaded to rouse itself if approached at the right moment with a well sunk Donegal Blue or a Jacob's Ladder.

The day seemed to be full of promise, as I can still remember, for the little river was clearing delightfully with the last round, creamy cakes of foam, which had been generated by the flood, now breaking away from tree roots and submerged branches, where they had been clinging, and spinning slowly downstream on a steadily diminishing water level. Less like full draught beer and more the delicate colour of a bottled lager, the current rippled clearly over shallows and on into a deeper run where my fly could still be seen swimming several inches below the surface.

I felt optimistic. There was that electric quality about the conditions which hinted momentous things might happen at any instant. I fished as carefully as I knew how, casting across and down, well under the far high bank where the current ran gently and where salmon tended to lie in the shadows waiting for whatever the stream might bring them.

Two or three more casts and there came a sudden swinging swirl beneath the bank with the gleam of a broad back breaking the surface. I felt no touch, however, for the fish missed the fly completely at its first attempt and returned to the river bottom to consider and perhaps try again.

With slow deliberation I retraced my steps a few yards upstream and, after a pause, cast over the same water again. Opposite the small patch of water celery where I had marked the salmon to lie it rose once more, majestically, head and tail gleaming steely-silver and this time as the waters closed upon it I felt that splendid weight and pull of a good fish firmly hooked.

At the instant when my ten-foot, split-cane rod bent to the salmon's first rush, and above the racing of the reel, I was aware of the sound of quickening steps behind me and a quiet word of congratulation at my shoulder. Peter, my companion for the day, on his way to join me from the pool above, had arrived most timely to offer any advice or material assistance that might be required. Peter was a thoughtful and careful fisherman and a considerable theoretician on angling matters - something which I could never claim to be. He was most scrupulous in the care of his tackle, preparing and checking it for each day's outing in an exemplary manner which I had noted but had never been able to copy.

My salmon came slowly towards us after the first few minutes of engagement and paused beneath the grass shelf where we both stood. Then, sensing our presence, it turned and fled down and across the full stretch of the Sandhole. Ten yards of line unwinding from the reel rapidly became twenty, twenty-five and then thirty, extending so quickly that the spliced attachment of casting line to backing became visible between my fingers.

I determined to increase control on the fish by raising my rod top further, gaining height and lessening the risk of my fly being shaken free. But line continued to stream through the rod eyes as the fish ran on regardless, finally reaching a narrow throat in the river where the pool tailed off over a bed of round stones before breaking into a series of heavy rapids. The force of water doubled the tension on my line. Another boiling swirl on the top with a glimpse of tail fin: tension grew so that drops of water flew like rain from the line; a dramatic shake and shudder transmitted through the length of the rod to my arm; another faint swirl - and then all was gone!

My rod straightened and pointed skywards, denuded of any vestige of line. All that remained was a short length of backing still wound around the reel. The braided silk had snapped just below the join and vanished completely into the river together with nylon cast, fly and salmon attached. Disconsolately I tested the yards of backing by pulling them between my hands: they parted as easily as stems of rotten grass.

Peter, I remember, was the soul of diplomacy and sympathy in his comments, not suggesting at the time what I knew as well as he to be the truth - that I should never have been on the river with tackle in such lamentable condition: a line suffering from too many years of use and rotten-through, probably on account of my failure to air and dry it after use in the past. More recently, however, with the lapse of intervening years, Peter has, not infrequently, reminded me sorrowfully of the event at the Sandhole, dwelling lengthily on the need to check tackle, on the probable size of the salmon lost and the undoubted inconvenience caused to it for some time afterwards by having to trail thirty yards of line around the river bed. On this last point I prefer to persuade myself that the fly would surely have come free once cast or line became inevitably wrapped around the first immovable rock or snag encountered. I hope so anyway.

Returning from the subject of rotten, uncared for fishing lines to the matter of landing nets, and problems which they can cause, it is well known that some nets are by design and construction infinitely less troublesome than others which are, in their behaviour, nothing but an abomination. As an example, the modern fully collapsible or folding net, despite its ingenuity, must always be regarded as a potential hazard capable of turning triumph into tragedy at a moment's notice. The theory behind the construction of a net of this sort is that it should collapse conveniently, at a finger touch, into a configuration which occupies minimal space and can hang comfortably at the angler's side or back without in any way obstructing his casting, whilst being ready for immediate action when unfolded by a quick shake or turn of the wrist.

Theory becomes practice with the best designed models but it is by no means to be relied upon as a generalization, in my experience. There is an example of what I have in mind, suspended ingloriously from a hook in our family tackle room, which has for many years, in the hands of my sons and myself, defied any number of deft shakes and turns of the wrist to bring it into its operational state when urgently required at the water's edge. Whenever this particular landing net has been on my back, in a collapsed state, its meshes have tended to congregate, secretively, into dense clusters at the corners of the supporting frame, from which position they could only be loosened by the use of both hands together or by employing one hand with one's teeth in combination, leaving the other hand to cope simultaneously with rod, reel and the resistance of a hooked fish being worked towards the bank. As a result there are times when I have been forced to lift a played-out trout from the water in, or rather upon, what resembled a sort of tennis racquet and lob it frantically onto dry land before the fish became unhooked.

An alternative to the folding type of net is a substantial long staff with a fixed frame which is permanently formed in rounded or pear shape and therefore always ready for action ashore or in a boat. When carried by the walking angler, however, it tends to restrict free movement, for the staff can get amongst one's legs and feet at crucial moments rather than assist progress. There is therefore always a temptation to relinquish a landing net of this kind at a succession of intermediate points on lake shore or river bank, with the intention that it can be reached in any case of sudden need. As a result I have lived to regret the several occasions when a lightly hooked fish has proved to be beyond reach of the place where my net was lying or when, in the anxiety of the moment, I was simply unable to find it amongst long grass or bushes where it lay hidden. An example of this carelessness fresh in my mind relates to the hooking of a salmon late into the dusk of a June evening on the River Drowes at Lareen. Too late I discovered that being on my own, I would have to 'walk' the fish some twenty yards up river to a point where dimly I could see my net lying at the water's edge. In the event the salmon firmly refused to 'walk' with me and in the ensuing struggle the fly came loose and the fish vanished unseen into the night.

Central, of course, to a fisherman's needs in the way of tackle is the fly rod, consideration and choice of which constitutes a subject on which whole books can and have been written. In my early, unmarried, days the greatest affection of which I was capable seems, on reflection, to have been devoted to a steel-centred, split-cane rod, made by Hardy Bros, which I then possessed. This lovely little nine foot rod I inherited in the early nineteen-forties from a cousin who died at Arnhem and who had himself fished with it since boyhood. Because of its family associations as much as its inherent delicacy of balance, remarkable strength and indefinable aesthetic qualities I could never at that time think of fishing with anything else so long as my split cane rod (a Hardy Brothers' 'Perfection') survived. It has been regularly revarnished, rebound where necessary, awarded a succession of green cloth containers, and given the place of honour in my tackle cupboard.

In terms of the number of fish played and landed perhaps its record is not so very great compared with those belonging to more successful or more constant fishermen whom I know. Nevertheless it has taken a vital part in most of my angling adventures over a quarter of a century, proving itself capable of dealing with some thirty or forty small salmon or grilse and a good few hundred trout of assorted sizes. Only in most recent years have I been compelled to accept that, despite the careful, complex structure and attention to detail found in good split cane rods, these have to be set against the extraordinary lightness-with-strength - and modest cost - of modern carbon fibre and other synthetic rods. I therefore load one of these new inventions into the car whenever I go fishing nowadays and put alongside it my old Perfection as 'first-reserve' or in case I feel the need for a change of weight or a brief reminder of the past.

With two- or three-piece rods there has always been a problem in assembling the pieces in such a way that the rod could be secure while in use but could also be taken apart at the end of the day by the effort of one person - without damage. Joints too tight were nevertheless better than joints too slack and careful greasing of metal ferrules was always better than the use of abrasives.

In fact I cannot recall that my old cane rods, Hardy or other makes, ever did come apart while fishing. Not so, regrettably, the synthetic weapons which we now possess. I have, on occasion seen the top half of my son's rod separate itself from the butt section and project like a harpoon at the water when he has been casting vigorously. Only the restraining presence of flies on the cast prevented the top from being lost in the lake. Similarly I have watched, with helpless concern, as the same son played a moderate size trout on his carbon fibre rod, the butt and reel only being under his control, while the detached upper portion of the rod closely pursued the fish beneath the lake surface before finally emerging, all somehow still interconnected. Of course a precautionary piece of adhesive tape wrapped around a joint serves to provide reasonable insurance against such happenings, whilst another piece will prevent the reel from quitting its mounting in moments of stress.

Lesser items of tackle than rods and nets have also contributed in their various ways to a quota of accidents in my personal fishing history. As regards the problems engendered by casts, or 'leaders' as they seem to be called now, I recollect clearly the days of silkworm 'gut' and all the bother associated with it: the essential ritual of soaking every length before any knot could be safely tied or a fly attached. Standard practice was the use of damping tins, with multi layers of odorous wet felt between which to store a made-up cast and its replacements needed for each day's fishing. Failure to follow the rules or to remove a cast from its moist confines before reaching a state of rottenness resulted in more than one break on the water and tragically lost fish.

Although I dislike the polyamide, nylon as yet another synthetic material belonging more properly to a chemical laboratory than to the riverside, I am bound to recognize its indisputable advantages of strength, longevity and convenient usage. Only as my fingers grow less nimble and my eyesight less certain have the difficulties of manipulating its fine, slippery strands into the semblance of a double blood-knot become acute. May I be forgiven for the number of occasions there have been, and for the things I have then said, when I was left to contemplate the curly end of a nylon dropper where a knot has failed to free a fly from the restraint of a distant weed or to prevent the departure of a good fish.

Hooks and flies attached to them in enormous variety embody as many reasons for catching fish, or not catching them, as there are difference in size, shape, colour, pattern and their behaviour in the water. I would not like to guess how many more trout I might have brought ashore in my lifetime if hook points had always been sharp and full barbs present. If flies had continued to float when that was required of them, or sunk promptly when they were supposed to be 'wet', how much greater perhaps would have been the number of rises attracted. I leave aside as too tedious for contemplation here, the detailed technology and entomology of fly patterns, and the far too frequently aired consideration of matching patterns to the presumed interests and inclinations of feeding fish. So far as the fish-catching value of an artificial fly is concerned I will only comment that, in my experience, some flies, obtained from some sources, have proved on trial to be better tied than others; some have resisted stoutly the action of wind, sun, water and the sharp teeth of trout over several seasons. Some, on the other hand, have disintegrated at the first encounter, unwinding long trails of hackle or ribbing to leave a naked hook, or else they have quickly declined from their original bright, shop-counter colours to a drab monochrome, following one or two bathes in lake or river.

In concluding this view of problems which have harassed my fishing experience I should refer, briefly, to the entanglement of casts. As is well known, this curse of the squally day, the dark evening, the confines of fishing three-in-a-boat, or merely the heedless moment, can suddenly beset any one of us. A tangle can, like clouds in the sky, take an infinity of forms and shapes, ranging in awfulness from a simple 'wind knot' (which can generally be undone by prodding with a pin), or the subtle inter-looping of dropper with adjacent dropper (which can generally be shaken free), to the absolutely unyielding five-star, bird's nest confusion of an entire three-fly cast and several yards of line together. For good measure it is likely that one or more of the flies will simultaneously be set fast in the landing net, in the boat timbers or in the back of the angler's jacket.

Such a situation understandably attracts the attentions of the humorist or cartoonist. To fishermen of my acquaintance, however, it comprises a form of frustration which more than any other mishap fully tests their supposedly exemplary patience.

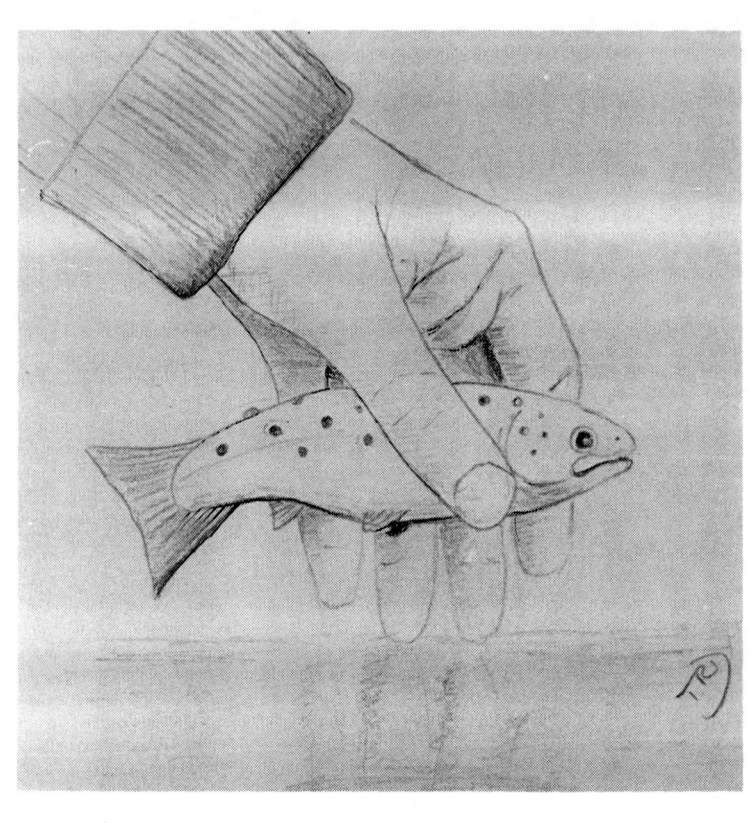

Small Fry

*"It has long been an axiom of mine that the little
things are infinitely the most important"*
(Conan Doyle)

In many fishing waters of my experience, particularly the acid, peaty loughs of the West of Ireland, it is a fact that trout may never grow larger than four to six ounces, despite their age, such is the poverty of feeding for them.

Because I have always had a great affection for small, remote, mountainy lakes in Fermanagh and Donegal where plant and insect life within the water is bare and lean compared to the larger, richer lakes further east, I have acquired a considerable knowledge of fish whose length has to be recorded in centimetres rather than inches and along whose diminutive flanks there is barely space to count a dozen speckles between gills and tail.

Like thumb prints, no two individual trout are identical in marking when they emerge fresh from the water - either in their colour or in the grouping and size of speckles. Little trout are remarkably beautiful to look at as well as being good to eat, except for those few individuals which have a tendency to large heads, lanky bodies and a muddy-white flesh.

Although trout are small in the loughs and streams which I

have in mind and natural feeding is limited, there is no certainty that they will always be eager to seize anything and everything offered by a fisherman. They can be as coy or choosey on occasion as larger, more sophisticated fish elsewhere.

Nevertheless, given a summer day with the right sky and the wind in the right quarter there is likely to be an enthusiastic response to the arrival of a fly fisherman with a team of Wickham's Fancy, Hare's Ear and Orange Grouse or a similar assortment made up from the more colourful corner of his fly box.

Sometimes there may even be an embarrassing level of success when a suicidal enthusiasm to take the fly is evident, regardless of pattern or presentation. In such circumstances some form of mental or practical adjustment by the angler is desirable.

With foresight this adjustment can be provided by ensuring that the adult angler is accompanied by a junior member of the family or friend for whom the novelty and delight of bringing home anything that swims has not yet worn off. In the rôle of instructor of 'ghillie' - and being prepared to assist frequently in the event of tangles and other hazards - one can relive a great deal of one's own youthful excitement. Further, while demonstrating how to cast, strike, hook, play and land, it is possible to justify a considerable amount of fishing on one's own account and to add substantially to the day's bag without comment or criticism.

If fish catching ever becomes too easy but one is unwilling to stop altogether and go home, a handicap element can even be introduced, perhaps by casting left-handed, by removing barbs from the flies, or by setting a minimal target of two fish on a cast at the same time.

More seriously, there is a useful opportunity on these days

spent amongst small trout, in the company of young anglers, to observe as well as teach the humanity in addition to technology of fishing.

All fish which are deliberately killed are to be taken home for cooking and eating; not discarded in a ditch when dead, or given to the cat to accept or ignore as it thinks fit.

Those fish which it is not intended to kill must be handled gently and returned to the water with the least possible shock to their system. We are at present attracting more than enough adverse criticism from the militantly humane on account of the supposed cruelty of our sport.

Much has been said by trout fishermen about the great sporting qualities of mountainy trout and this is given as an excuse for the hours spent by grown men who skirmish amongst reed beds and water lilies at a remote lough side for prey so small that at first strike they are likely to quit the water and fly over one's head into the heather behind.

It is at this point, and especially when observed by younger or female members of the family, that there is nothing else for it but to adjust one's spectacles and, on hands and knees, creep amongst tussocks of peat and sedge grass to discover where the tiny catch has landed. Eventually - for it is surprising how long a fish can survive out of water - having wiped and readjusted glasses a half-dozen times, the slight trembling of a stem, or the glint of silver at its base will reveal the presence. With one's hands cupped as though to contain a breath of air the trout must then be carried back to the lake and lowered - not thrown - back to its home. With luck and, with gentle prodding by any children who happen to be present, it rights itself in the water, gills and tail flutter steadily and then, suddenly, it is gone.

Rod and line can be disentangled from the heather, hooks

inspected and fishing resumed. It may be wise, however, to move along the bank by some twenty yards or so in case the same small fish should choose to repeat its startling experience.

I know of a comfortable family-fishing hotel in the North-West of Scotland which, justifiably, publishes for its clientele the scenic attractions of a group of lochs which it owns, scattered over the surrounding 'forest'. Some of the lochs, as I recall, lie close at hand to the house, maybe a half-mile distant; others are remote and require of the enthusiast a very considerable trek of three or four miles along rough paths through the Cromarty Hills.

The hotel brochure, at the time I recall, spoke impressively of large numbers of trout to be found in its lochs, of the trouts' fondness for a Blue Zulu, or an Invicta or a Butcher (or indeed for anything with feathers that you might care to offer them). It also expounded on the extreme hardiness and sportfulness of the fish when hooked. A large, round tray was placed daily in the hotel porch for the purposes of displaying the successes of fishermen who had returned sweaty but triumphant after a day's work on its waters.

I felt insufficiently energetic to attempt the far-off lochs, which were pointed out to me on the hotel map, and contented myself instead with a day booked on one of the 'home' waters. A small, flat-bottomed dinghy was available to carry my wife and myself from end-to-end of Loch na Greibe. Without a keel or the precaution of a sea anchor our progress was fast, furious and largely unmanageable in front of a stiff breeze coming in from the neighbouring Atlantic.

Sally struggled valiantly with the oars while I tempted the trout with a varied and colourful assortment of flies. The trout were here, there and everywhere, and by no means disturbed by some untidy casting which raised little fountains of water whenever flies landed heavily above their heads, or when oar blades made a false stroke.

A small party of red deer, as I remember, were more alarmed than the fish by our endeavours and after examining us nervously from a vantage point on the leeward shore they made off at speed for the safety of higher slopes.

Trout continued to come happily to the fly. Indeed they came happily to any fly, two together on several occasions, tail fly, bob fly or centre; on the surface or beneath it. Fish brought into the boat would have weighed, I suppose, four ounces or five ounces or maybe, though rarely, six. There was not a genuine half-pounder amongst them and nothing it seemed that I could dare bring back with us for the awful dignity of the round tray in the hotel.

Eventually after searching every corner of the twenty acre loch we gave up rowing and drifting and fishing, exercised but somewhat disappointed. Fish never gave up rising throughout our stay on the water.

Once back at the hotel we attempted an inconspicuous passage via the back door towards our room. The manager observed us, however, through his office door and smiled enquiringly. Had we had luck? Had we not brought back fish? A pity - and surprising! The London party just returned after an overnight camp at Loch na Southan (the most remote of all the lakes) had done well and returned with a dozen nice trout.

Deeply conscious of my incompetence I followed my wife to the porch to see what it was that I had to match.

We gazed at the tray. Sprinkled over it in artistic distribution, like dark leaves floating on a silver pond were twelve trout whose total weight I would have confidently assessed as being in the region of three pounds. They were identical in size with those from Loch na Greibe. A beautifully hand written white card alongside gave details of fly patterns and sizes used, the direction and force of the wind, the time of day when caught and the exact temperature of the water. It concluded with the names of the four members of the party who had participated and the date. I felt distinctly better.

In some cases, of course, small fish would grow to a much greater size if given the chance, and problems in salmon rivers are well known, where parr or smolts are a constant nuisance to any fly fishermen, particularly in conditions of low water. Despite their frantic inclinations to perish on the hook these little animals require to be treated with mercy and the solicitude due to their being miniatures of splendid fish which might one day return to the same river and provide some fortunate person with a memorable experience.

It is hard always to be high-principled with salmon parr. I confess to occasions of irritation and brusque reaction as, for example, when a six inch long fish seized a shrimp fly in front of the nose, as I imagined it, of a heavy sea trout for whom it was properly intended. The resultant chaotic splashing, accompanied by the overhanging shadow of my presence when I was forced to stand up and separate the offending parr from a tuft of rushes must have sent any sensitive sea trout into immediate flight. Only the parr remained gasping and apologetic at my feet, but more or less unscathed and expecting immediate release.

Since it is by no means possible to recognize the size of a fish when it seizes the fly underwater, or even rises to take it near the surface, much ill founded excitement is caused by hungry little sprats enlivening, to a degree, what could otherwise be a blank day.

On the other hand, as is well known, a small rise is not always that of a small fish, and a minute dimple on the calm water of a lake at dusk, suggestive of a hatching fly or a raindrop, has in the memory of many anglers been suddenly transformed into a massive swirl and hectic rush when a large trout was hooked.

There was one such instance for me several years ago on Lough Eske which was unusual enough to deserve particular mention and it illustrates very well the difficulties of determining the size of fish while they are still in the water.

I was drifting by myself, in one of Scott Swan's boats, along the line of a sunken ridge which runs east from the north side of Castle Bay towards Pigeon Island. The breeze must have been light and the sun shining for I remember that I could see quite clearly brown rocks sliding beneath the keel at a depth of two or three feet. The solid shadow of the boat crept slowly before me, almost certainly putting to flight any lurking sea trout.

Not so the local population of little brownies, however, which skipped and slapped happily at any fly which came within their sight. I must have caught three or four and returned them to the lake. A minor diversion was the inclusion of a char, smaller even than the brown trout, but more attractive in its marking. Char, although infrequently seen by anglers in the summer months, are plentiful in deeper parts of the lough and in autumn they move in shoals close into the east shore where, by long established tradition, local people fish for them with bait, subsequently drying and salting their catch for food in the winter.

Presently, as the boat drifted on and near to Pigeon Island, another small trout rose to my fly, was hooked and came immediately clear of the water, showing all of its six inches length before vanishing again. There followed several seconds of jigging at the line before I prepared to lift cast and fish unceremoniously into the boat.

As my rod was raised, however, there was a sudden increase in tension on the line which then rushed violently through the water, drawing several yards from the reel. The rod tip now bent sharply and ominously towards a point some oar's length away from the bows.

By standing up I was able to see more clearly into the water where the line ran steeply downwards. It seemed to me probable that my fly had been taken down to the bottom where it had fouled a sunken branch or a stone, magnifying the resistance offered by the little fish which I had seen. Or perhaps while it hung on the bob fly a second trout had taken the tail fly. Or again, perhaps a trout was foul hooked and able to exert a pull out of proportion to its weight.

Now, however, by peering down into the lake water I could see what in fact had happened. The original trout, which I had already seen, had been hooked by the top fly on the three-fly cast. It remained securely attached to that fly, and it in turn was now gripped by another trout, substantially larger, which held its prey determinedly across the back and with apparently no intention of letting go.

I had, in a sense, hooked two fish simultaneously on one fly - a circumstance which was something new in my experience and unlikely to continue for much longer as soon as the larger, cannibal fish became aware of my threatening presence overhead.

There was little to be done except watch. The larger fish continued, visibly, to swim to and fro, pulling against the resistance of my rod, but not feeling the hook which was embedded in the jaws of the smaller trout. Then, inevitably, after a minute the cannibal relaxed its jaws, perhaps to get a fresh grip, and its prey fluttered to the surface - still attached to my fly.

A second later and without any movement on my part, the ascending tail fly had stuck fast in the cannibal fish before it could turn away. The hook was lodged in its side, below the dorsal fin.

An extremely awkward period of playing both trout together followed with the larger fish, now alarmed, running more of less where it liked and trailing its small companion to and fro like a rag doll tied to a dog's tail. Eventually, both grew tired and floated to the top, on their sides, so that with one sweep of my landing net I was able to gather them together and deposit them safely in the bottom of the boat.

Once netted and laid at my feet the cannibal trout proved to be impressive neither in weight nor in beauty. It weighed, I guessed, rather less than two pounds, with a dark, black head and a lean, heavily spotted body, suggesting that the fish had had to work hard over the summer for whatever it could find to satisfy its unsociable diet.

On impulse I returned the big fish, with the little one, alive to the lake where they swam away, thoughtfully, it seemed, in opposite directions.

This somewhat macabre incident involving a very small trout contrasts with most of my experiences in the lilliputian world to which I have been referring, and which tend to be associated more with streams and mountainy rivers than with lakes. Running water has always been more attractive to me than still water and miniature waterfalls, miniature rapids and circling pools not ten feet across have been for me perfect replicas of what fishermen like most in grander rivers.

Most grown men at some time or other, and more especially

as they get older, like to return in memory, if not in fact, to a world where little things and minor events were adequate for their needs. This is particularly so for a fisherman. At three score years he can happily shed two score of them, or more, and approach with renewed pleasure places where water rarely gets above his knees and where, in a momentary return to youthful vigour, he can even jump dry shod from bank to opposite bank at the narrowest channels.

Here, under overhanging tufts of heather and behind washed heads of granite lie a size of fish sufficient for his mood. With a fine cast and a small dark fly and a short rod, perhaps discarded from more serious work, he can be happily employed.

I repeat what I said earlier however, namely that the pleasures of the day are enhanced and indeed one's preoccupation excused if the fisherman is fortunate enough to have as company some young member of the family for whom there is a novelty and a newness about it all and who has the same liking for the surroundings as one had oneself in the dreamy days of youth.

Pause for Food

"A man hath no better thing than to eat and to drink and to be merry"
                    (Ecclesiastes Ch 8 v15)

Attention to eating and drinking does not take up much space in present day books on fishing. Being merry may not be regarded as quite in the spirit of the sport and is left by most people to that time of day when catching fish, or not catching them, has finished and there is an opportunity for relaxation at home, or better still in some comfortable hostelry.

To eat and to drink satisfactorily, however, during the course of a day's fishing is in my opinion an essential part of the total experience and not merely something to be fitted in as an after thought. My view, developed over half a century of fishing - including very many blank days and empty bags, are that the non-fishing half-hours or hours spent for lunch and tea breaks have, in retrospect, been amongst the most pleasant in memory. Critics might suggest that if these breaks had been shortened, or been fewer in number, my catches would have been substantially greater. Indeed, this may be.

To decide when to eat and where to eat during a day's angling has always been more important to me than what was actually to be eaten. Whenever the time for lunch approaches an angler is most likely to find himself in some place which is far removed from shops or restaurants. What is to be eaten or drunk has, therefore, been arranged several hours previously. There is no choice.

The proper time for taking lunch requires careful consideration and if two or more people are involved, in a boat or on the bank, agreement is not easily arrived at. The principal factors to be weighed are: first, the intensity of one's hunger, or an awareness of the lapse of time since breakfast, and a calculation of the hours still to pass before the next proper meal can be expected. With this may be linked the particular attraction of some content of the lunch bag - like a barbecued cold chicken or a bottle of Moselle which has replaced the usual cans of beer.

A second factor may be the degree of success which has already been achieved on the water: the comforting presence of a number of good fish lying on the bottom boards of the boat, or on the grass, where they can be contemplated with satisfaction while lunch is being taken. Conversely, there may be an indigestible worry that one could be losing the best rise - or the only rise - of the day by quitting the water when one does.

Thirdly, there is the question of weather conditions. An interlude of flat calm, the onset of hurricane force winds or a torrential downpour may enforce a break from fishing anyway and make one glad to spend time instead attempting to build a picnic fire or boil a kettle.

The appropriate moment for lunch may also be determined by the fact of having arrived at a place which by its nature seems particularly suitable. At the conventional hour of one o'clock it often happens that one's boat is drifting steadily across a lough halfway, perhaps, between two distant shores. By waiting for a further half hour, however, the boat is likely to be abreast of a sheltered bay, with a sandy beach and protecting trees extending a timely invitation to pull ashore and rest awhile.

If the precise time of day and the state of the weather are of no great consequence, and there is opportunity to choose the ideal lunch site, then care should be taken. As regards the ground on which one is to rest and spread oneself: my personal preference has always been, where possible, for heather banks, in flower or otherwise, spring, summer or autumn. No matter what its age or state of growth there is a dry, wiry, springy luxury about heather unrivalled by any other natural surface that I know of. I could become poetic on the subject. Grass, fallen trees, sand and rocks - all bear no comparison.

When seeking protection from wind and driving rain during lunch the obvious preference is for a lee shore rather than one to windward. Otherwise a boat drawn up on stones, no matter how carefully, will be a disturbance to one's peace of mind by the tendency for its hull to squeak and complain against neighbouring stones with every gust of wind and incoming waves. An important proviso, however, about beaching on lee shores is that even in apparent shelter from wind a boat should be secured with absolute certainty to a tree branch or a substantial rock. Left to its own devices and even partially afloat, after the disembarking of fishermen and gear, a sixteen foot boat can develop a life of its own and steal secretly adrift. With remarkable speed under a slight offshore breeze it may only be discovered when at a distance beyond even the longest waders and presenting an urgent challenge to some strong swimming member of the party. I have known this happen.

Another requirement which has always been important to me when selecting a site for lunch or tea is that it should provide a good view of the water. Even when one is seated or recumbent the near stretches of lake or river should be clearly in sight. Otherwise there will be a constant niggle at the back of one's mind: a taking fish might start to move within casting distance at the very moment when soup is being poured or sandwiches unwrapped. Repeated standing up and walking about to take a look and sitting down again is not conducive to relaxed digestion and merely results in cups being knocked over or tackle or food being trodden underfoot.

As a generalization it might be said that whenever fishing picnics are to be enjoyed there should be a peaceful, quiet environment free from the chance of any intrusion. At risk of seeming antisocial I would always try to find a few acres, at least, all to myself, or reserved for my companions of the day. No other angler should be within earshot, preferably, and if possible none within sight, especially in case he be observed taking a good fish while we are temporarily out of action.

My friends and I are particularly likely to be upset, when lunching, by the sight of others who are not conforming to civilised standards of care and thoughtfulness in the disposal of their litter. Sadly, the accumulation of plastic wrappers, shattered beer bottles and empty cans, which now desecrates so many lovely Irish waters seems to have increased in greater measure than the number of people fishing. Such pollution is so completely unnecessary and illustrative of a heedless attitude towards all that the countryside has to offer to present and future generations of fishermen that I can find no reason or possible excuse for it.

Despite the importance of farm animals and their unquestionable right to be a part of many fishing localities, I prefer to be free from their company at lunchtime. A substantial fence should be between the fishing party and any herds of cattle which may be in the neighbourhood. Although almost always friendly in disposition and at worst playful, young bullocks or heifers can show their intense interest in visiting fishermen in a restless and disturbing way. This interest reaches a peak whenever lunchtime is accompanied by the lighting of a picnic fire. The crackle of flames and the plume of smoke arising from dead twigs, maybe flavoured with the aroma of frying, rather than deterring the advance of cattle, as it might do to wilder animals, seems to draw them nearer in a hypnotized circle. Large, clumsy feet can fall disastrously on unguarded gear. A fly rod leant carefully against a tree may not be trampled upon but dropper flies dangle at a height which coincides with switching tails and tossing heads. My younger son once had line drawn from his reel by a self-hooked thirty-stone bullock faster than by any fish he ever encountered. The cast broke almost immediately and we suppose that the beast, if it were still alive today would be carrying a small March Brown deep in its shaggy coat.

Even the amiable and more predictable milk cow may approach a lunch party too closely if she considers that there is something around which merits investigation. I recollect once having a slobbery tug-of-war with a large Friesian cow who disputed possession of a green fabric rod container. The cow had picked it up from the grass as being distinctly grass like and three parts swallowed it before I realized what was happening and managed to lay a firm hold of the free end. It was an incident that spoiled lunch for me and, presumably, also for the cow.

Rocks abound at the surrounds of most Irish loughs, more so than trees, and, when flat or moss-covered, can serve admirably as seats as well as tables. The great limestone slabs lying around Loughs Erne, Mask, Conn and Cullen suggest by their shape and arrangement that they were designed expressly for the convenience of anglers' picnics. A variety of holes and hollows worn in their upper surfaces, by the action of water and smaller stones together, provide all that could be desired for holding the furnishing of a picnic - cups, plates, bottles, a clutch of hard-boiled eggs, thermos flask etc.

There was one particular meal which comes to my mind when hard-boiled eggs, tomatoes, apples and other 'rolling' items figured prominently. John, his father and I had been fishing Lough Rushen in South Donegal during the morning, but forsook the lake shore for drier ground when it came time for a mid-day break. We made our way back to a lane by which the lake is approached at the north end but which had become choked with intermingling willow bushes so that there was no apparent throughway for wheeled traffic. Not even tractor wheels marked the road's unmetalled sandy surface and it was scoured clean by the summer's passing showers and breezes. Where we were a cluster of little dried out puddle holes were dotted around and as we unpacked lunch one hollow served to accommodate the tomatoes, another the eggs, a third the apples and so on. In between stood kettle, plates, mugs and other hardware, neatly disposed. The total effect as we sat down amongst it was colourful and convenient, occupying as it did the full width of the lane but with everything in reach and visible at a glance. A little group of beer bottles stood like skittles in the centre: alongside them a paper bag of scones with butter adjacent ready for spreading. Knives and spoons, always liable to be mislaid in grass or heather, were conspicuously at hand. We were organized and we were relaxed.

Without warning there suddenly appeared an elderly man riding a bicycle. He emerged from the bushy part of the road, fifty yards away, where we had thought there was no passage for any vehicle. His course was slow, wavering but emphatic and he showed no sign of stopping as he approached the assembly of obstacles in his path. Since there was no time to move ourselves, let alone the picnic materials, we watched in fascination as the bicycle threaded a sinuous way around and amongst the assortment on the lane. Not a tomato was bruised or a cup overturned by its passage. The teaspoons remained exactly where they had been but with a delicately defined tyre mark now separating them from the knives. The rustle of wheels on the soft road surface and an occasional click of the bicycle chain were the only sounds as we sat there in contemplation.

Once he had negotiated the last outlying thermos flask the old man acknowledged our presence, without turning his head, by a quiet observation to us on the fineness of the day and, after a few more pedal strokes, a confident expression as to the suitability of conditions for catching trout. He then passed gently out of sight beyond another screen of bushes and we returned to our lunch.

The actual composition of lunch or tea which is consumed on a day's fishing has never much concerned me. In summary, I have enjoyed over the years a wide variety of rolls, sandwiches, biscuits, pies and fruit, and things fried on wood fires, as well as a comprehensive range of drinks, hot and cold. The credit in this matter goes always to my wife whose imagination and care for detail has made me an object of envy amongst fishing friends.

One thing which I cannot claim to having ever enjoyed at the waterside has been the cooking and eating of freshly caught fish. In fact I think that the only time when I attempted something of this kind was shortly after reading a chapter written by Thomas Barker, two centuries ago, in which he dwelt upon the unequalled tastiness of small trout cooked in the ashes of a wood fire and eaten within an hour of catching.

John and I had succeeded in catching four or five half pound fish in a morning on Lough Conn and at one o'clock we had already lit a strong fire for the purpose of boiling a kettle and making ourselves warm. A day-old copy of the Irish Times lay in the boat and it occurred to us suddenly that here was an opportunity to test the romantic theory of on-the-spot, open-air fish cooking.

Trout were beheaded, cleaned out and carefully washed in the lake and then wrapped in sheets of damp newspaper, fold upon fold, before being thrust into the depths of the fire in the manner recommended.

Perhaps it was because the trout in their incinerated wrappings soon looked much like the remnants of burning sticks and were tossed somewhat rudely around as we mended the fire. Perhaps the wrapping paper was too dry, or too wet, or of insufficient thickness, or else the fire was too hot or too cold. At any event, in the end the charred and bony fragments which we recovered and were finally able to separate, approximately, from cocoons of ashy paper provided one of the least pleasant eating experiences which I wish to ever recall. We offered some pieces to the boatman who had been taking his own sandwiches a short distance away and I still remember the positive nature of his refusal and his observation that cooking was best left to the wife and to the proper convenience of a kitchen.

Sea Trout At Fourteen

*"Angling may be said to be so like the
mathematics that it can never be fully learnt"*
                                        (Walton)

Most fishermen would agree that to experience a good day with sea trout while still in one's early teens is a very fortunate and memorable thing. So far as I was concerned, the opportunity to catch sea trout did not arise until well into my twenties and before that time I had to be content with brown trout of modest size, and a very occasional small salmon.

Quite recently, however, I was able to participate in a day when my elder son, aged fourteen, had his first proper encounter with sea trout in Donegal.

It was early in August and there had been substantial rain up in the Bluestack mountains, on and off, over several days. A score of feeder streams, heavy with spate water, tumbled noisily into Lough Eske, raising its level by several inches and spreading dark stains of peat wherever they entered.

By nine o'clock in the morning the clouds had lifted their trailing skirts clear of Tawnawilly to the north and were breaking up here and there under pressure from a mild but steady breeze.

Colin and I had left the car below Scott Swan's house and

headed across the lake with the wind behind us, confident in the knowledge that, at that hour, we would have first honour on the water. We made a course straight for the Ridge.

Presently, having rounded the corner of O'Donnell's island, the boat was following, approximately, the river current which creeps slowly from the Ridge to its outflow point half-a-mile away in Church Bay. In July, August and even September this channel forms a busy roadway for large numbers of sea trout which, once they have entered the lake, are inclined to follow it closely before scattering to their favourite lies.

We reached the place for which we had been heading in a few minutes more. The Ridge is an area not easily definable to a stranger and unless he takes soundings with an oar blade to check depth and feel the crunch of gravel underneath he may be fishing too close to the shore or too far from it. The best part of the water covers little more than an acre around the fringes of a sandy bed which gives the Ridge its name and which has been piled up and scattered again over centuries at the mouth of the Clogher river.

We prepared to fish. Since, in the opinion of my family, I am a difficult person to satisfy in a boat - speed, balance and exact position are rarely as I want them - I am generally required to take the oars myself. Colin settled himself in the stern.

The strength and direction of the wind were favourable to us, promising a steady drift parallel to the shore line and likely to cross the inflowing current at right angles.

Our bob flies skipped briskly over the wave tops while tail flies swam stealthily through the amber water a foot below the surface.

After a short spell of drifting and fishing I glanced across at my son's casting, wondering whether we might complete a half-hour without mutual entanglement or similar embarrassment.

At that instant the first trout of the day slashed swiftly at my fly and was gone again. Even while I was condemning myself for inattention the same fish, or its neighbour rose once more and was firmly hooked.

There followed minutes of excitement as line fled from the reel and was recovered again; silvery, twisting leaps and frantic dashes to get beneath the boat; anxious moments for both of us before at last the landing net could be used and the trout brought on board.

That fish, like two more which I caught soon after it on the same drift, was something between a pound and a pound-and-a-half in weight. I missed another and I saw a grilse of considerable size turning in the water close to my line.

It seemed that I was striking that particularly happy combination of light, wind, water level and a fishy state of mind which affected the sea trout as though they had been swimming five miles from Donegal Bay with the sole intention of committing suicide on my rod.

Colin and I shared the same assortment of fly patterns: Claret and Mallard, Black Pennell and Golden Olive. They had served me well enough for Lough Eske trout for the past twenty years and, so far as I was concerned, they were still adequate for any occasion.

But for the younger fisherman half-an-hour is a long time to spend without a fish, or even a rise, especially if one's father, for no obvious reason is wreaking havoc at the other end of the boat. It began to look dreadfully like one of those days when results are completely lop-sided and the fates decide that one person out of two will enjoy all the fun while his partner can only look on and wish.

Colin tried valiantly to continue his congratulations on my success whenever I hooked a fish and suppressed his sighs, more or less, while his own part of the lake remained undisturbed. My old Hardy rod seemed to draw the trout like a magnet that morning. His own fibre glass weapon stayed untested.

I broke a silence which had begun to hang heavily about us. "Here, try a few casts with my rod while I hold the boat in this line of foam. They seem to like my flies for some reason."

"No, no, Dad. It's all right," he said, though the sentiment was belied by a face of gloom. "It doesn't matter. Anyhow, I couldn't cast properly with it."

There followed a slightly irritated and untidy cast with his own rod. "You catch them. I'm OK."

Some more tactful persuasion on my part followed, with weakening counter-argument, until at last, with an air of resignation, Colin took the cane rod and, after a few tentative false casts, projected a short line behind the boat. I turned into the drift so that his line was now before him in the water.

A brief pause ensued while the black pennell scurried though the twilight beneath the waves.

Then with a marvellous suddenness there was a sweeping silver swirl on the top of the water, followed by a shout from the stern of the boat.

"I've got one, Dad...I've got a big one."

I remember that unfortunate sea trout as though it had been yesterday. It did all that a fresh-run, three-pound fish might do and reasonably expect to escape: hither and thither in front of us forty yards away, and then at arm's length with slack line all over the place; clean under the stern of the boat and up on the other side, jumping practically in amongst us. It was a three hundred and sixty degree tour which defeated my attempts to maintain any sort of status quo between boat and fish and which drove my son frantic with anxiety.

We had drifted ashore and two hundred yards eastward before Colin's sea trout was finally netted and dispatched. It was necessary thereupon to land and to lay the fish, with its smaller brethren, all re-washed and wiped, on the grass where it could be properly admired and compliments exchanged.

Willow wrens sang sweetly in the hazel bushes behind us and the sun shone brilliantly through a gap in the clouds. My son's face was a match for it in cheerful brightness.

We continued to fish thereafter and the morning was, by any standards, remarkable for its success.

Colin's next trout - to his own rod now - rose from the lake and then descended again, like a swallow on to the fly, just as he was recovering his line to make another cast. He followed that, ten minutes later, with a fish that took deep down at a moment when his rod had been rested on the side of the boat and the flies had sunk nearly to the lake bottom. Both fish were around a pound weight and were brought in with comparatively few alarms.

I also played my part and at one point rose what might have been as large a sea trout as Colin's. It was at a time, however, when we were practically aground to the windward of a cluster of rocks so that I was holding my rod over my left shoulder while struggling with both oars alternately.

For another hour there was no moment when we were without a sense of the nearness of sea trout and always there was the imminent expectation of a sudden rise or a strong pull under water.

When we finally reeled in and put down our rods a little after midday there were eleven sea trout between us, from three-quarters of a pound to three pounds. Several fish had grown dark from weeks' stay in the lake but most, including the largest, were still glittering with sea silver and might have left the tide below Donegal town only a few hours before.

I straightened the bows of the boat towards the west, at the end of our last drift across the Ridge.

Colin enthusiastically took my place at the oars and set himself for the row home. The breeze freshened slightly and small waves tapped softly against us whilst I reclined comfortably on the dry bottom boards with my back against a seat.

Both rods rested triumphantly alongside a landing net to which fish scales still adhered. Sea trout gleamed damply around my feet and I was able, through half closed eyes, to survey my partner's expression, pink with exertion and success.

A Companion On The River

"An excellent angler and now with God"
(Walton)

This memory of the River Erne, on the south borders of County Donegal, was passed on to me by an old friend whose knowledge of that lovely river, as it used to be, extends back further and with greater accuracy than my own.

It concerns that stretch of the Erne known to local people as 'the Wings', some two miles downstream from Belleek and at one time famous not only for its commercial eel fishing but also for the incomparable quality of trout angling which could be enjoyed there during summer evenings.

A herringbone arrangement of low stone walls, or weirs, leading towards a number of eel traps distributed across the width of the river, gave the place its name. All have now vanished under thirty feet of water - a part of the lower of two dams which government, in its wisdom, has constructed to provide for electricity generation in place of fishing.

A narrow, winding and ancient lane used to lead down to the Wings, on the South side, from the county road, and this gave access to the river for fishermen, as well as providing for a small monastery and chapel which used to overlook the water. Only weed-grown stumps of wall and loose heaps of half-dressed stones remained as evidence of any buildings. Even these, like the Wings, have now disappeared underwater.

My friend's story was about one particular evening, amongst others in July, when he had driven his car down the narrow lane as far as it would allow, skirting around the ruins and stopping only a few yards short of the river bank.

Conditions boded well for fishing. Soft-winged flies scrambling in the evening air were the prey not only for a colony of bats hawking to and fro over the water but also for occasional hungry trout which could be seen already splashing in quiet parts of the current. Fishing time would be limited, however, by failing light and Michael did not delay in putting his tackle together and exchanging shoes for thigh waders.

Once that was done, with bag and net slung across his back, he stepped from the overhanging grass bank down on to the nearest of the walls, its moss-covered stones barely a foot above the rippling current.

Within a few minutes of making his first cast two good-sized fish had risen to the fly, close-in to the weir, where a strong stream issued through gaps between the stones. Both flurried wildly on the surface and were gone without being hooked. This was followed by a period of some twenty minutes during which nothing stirred.

Further along the wall, where it slanted obliquely across the river, a combination of several small streams flowed together at a point well beyond casting distance, before flattening into an attractive ripple which ran parallel to an exposed gravel bed. Past experience drew Michael's attention to this place and since he knew the depth of the river he was able to step down off the weir and wade gently towards it.

The change proved worthwhile for after a few casts his tail

fly was taken violently by a heavy fish which fought furiously and silently in the dark water, taking line out to the deep water and then returning towards him, several times over. Finally, when it seemed to be tiring, the trout fled upstream and passed close by, heading for the weir above.

There, as the fish flapped wearily in the shadow of the stones, Michael became aware for the first time that he was not alone. Where he had been standing earlier on the weir another angler was now present, motionless, while watching intently the playing of the fish. If he had uttered any word it was not audible above the steady rustling of the river all around.

The newcomer held a fishing rod in one hand, but carried no net. Without hesitation, however, at the proper moment he stooped down to the water's edge and grasping the exhausted trout neatly behind the gills, threw it up on to the stones, before rapping it sharply so that it lay still.

The fly was disengaged and allowed to float back towards Michael who called out his thanks while starting to retrace his steps to the weir.

The stranger nodded gently and waved with his free hand in a gesture that seemed almost as much a benediction as an acknowledgement. However, apparently disinclined for conversation, or else anxious to continue his own fishing without delay he continued on his way along the top of the weir, casting as he went.

My friend had an impression of someone unusually tall and whose slender build was emphasized by the clinging, light-coloured coat which he wore, extending to below his knees. It was gathered at the waist by a belt or cord to which a sort of old fashioned tackle creel was attached. The rod which he worked back and forth through the darkening air was of a length uncommon even for Erne fishermen and reminded Michael of an antique style of green heart salmon rod for which the experts of earlier generations required strong wrists and a sensitive touch to operate with any success. Without any hat or cap the man's face was nevertheless barely distinguishable at a distance. Whether he was bearded or not the high collar of his coat made it impossible to be sure.

There remained not many yards between that part of the weir and the point where it ended abruptly at an open eel trap. Beyond there nobody would be able to wade the powerful, centre current of the Erne or to cross from one weir to the next. Generally it was a place not much fished for trout because of the weight and speed of the water.

However, Michael could still make out the other angler near the furthest part of the wall, casting steadily into the rushing water below, and the concentrated study with which he applied himself suggested a person who knew very well what he was about.

Before any further success could be seen or achieved by either man a change took place in the evening. A light, chill breeze suddenly crept over the river from the north-west and in a moment its breath had swept away the flies dancing above the current. It made a plaything of those mist patches which till then had rested over the neighbouring, low lying fields. Grey shreds gathered and twisted across the Wings as though they had an energy of their own. One small nucleus of mist hung momentarily in an inverted cone around the place where the tall fisherman stood, seeming to increase in density so that he almost vanished from view, with only head and shoulders remaining faintly visible, his movements barely distinguishable from the swirling of the mist.

Michael gathered up his trout where it had been left for him.

By torchlight he could see that it was above average size, even for the Wings. Nearer three pounds than two, it was short and deep like all Erne trout and with a gleam of silver overlying a dense pattern of gold and red spots.

It seemed, however, certain to be the only fish of the night, so chill had the air now become and so completely had the flies on which, a little earlier, trout had been feeding hungrily vanished.

Making his way carefully along the uneven top of the weir my friend was back once more on the river bank in a few minutes and at the side of his car in a few more. Then, after his rod and line had been taken down, his tackle tidied away and boots exchanged for shoes he was able to take his seat in the car and prepare to drive off.

The instant Michael switched on the car headlamps they cast their full beam across the river in front of him and along the length of the weir where he had been walking and fishing a few minutes earlier. The harsh light was an intrusion into the solitude of the place and the deep shadows which it cast here and there made the pools seem blacker and the stones rougher than by daylight. He thought of the fisherman still out in the weir and reached for the switch to dim the lights.

But even as Michael did so, with the Wings still bathed in light and every feature revealed within a hundred yards of the car, it was clearly apparent that there was no longer any person to be seen on the weir, or near it. The river was, except for himself, deserted.

It did not seem possible that any accident could have happened. There had been no cry or sound of any kind and Michael was convinced that his companion of the evening knew his way and knew the river as well as he did himself. As to how the stranger had vanished he could only suppose that somehow, in a moment's inattention on his own part, the other had managed to overtake and pass him unseen and unheard between the river bank and the car. Michael turned the car and drove away.

At home the following morning he responded to his mother's enquiries about the evening's fishing by showing her the one trout which he had brought back, explaining that a sudden chill breeze had prevented his getting a better bag.

She agreed: "Even here there was a sharp sort of air late on, and a wet mist around the low part of the garden, with only the tops of the apple trees showing. Not a nice, soft summer night, at all."

'Your father used to be disappointed by odd evenings like that when he went to the Wings in the old days."

"He would joke that evenings like that were only fit for the monks from the little monastery to be out fishing - and he would swear to me that he had seen one of them once, practically alongside of him, casting away, off the weir."

"A nice quiet man he said, with a great way of landing trout without a net."